ANGEL™

Autumnal

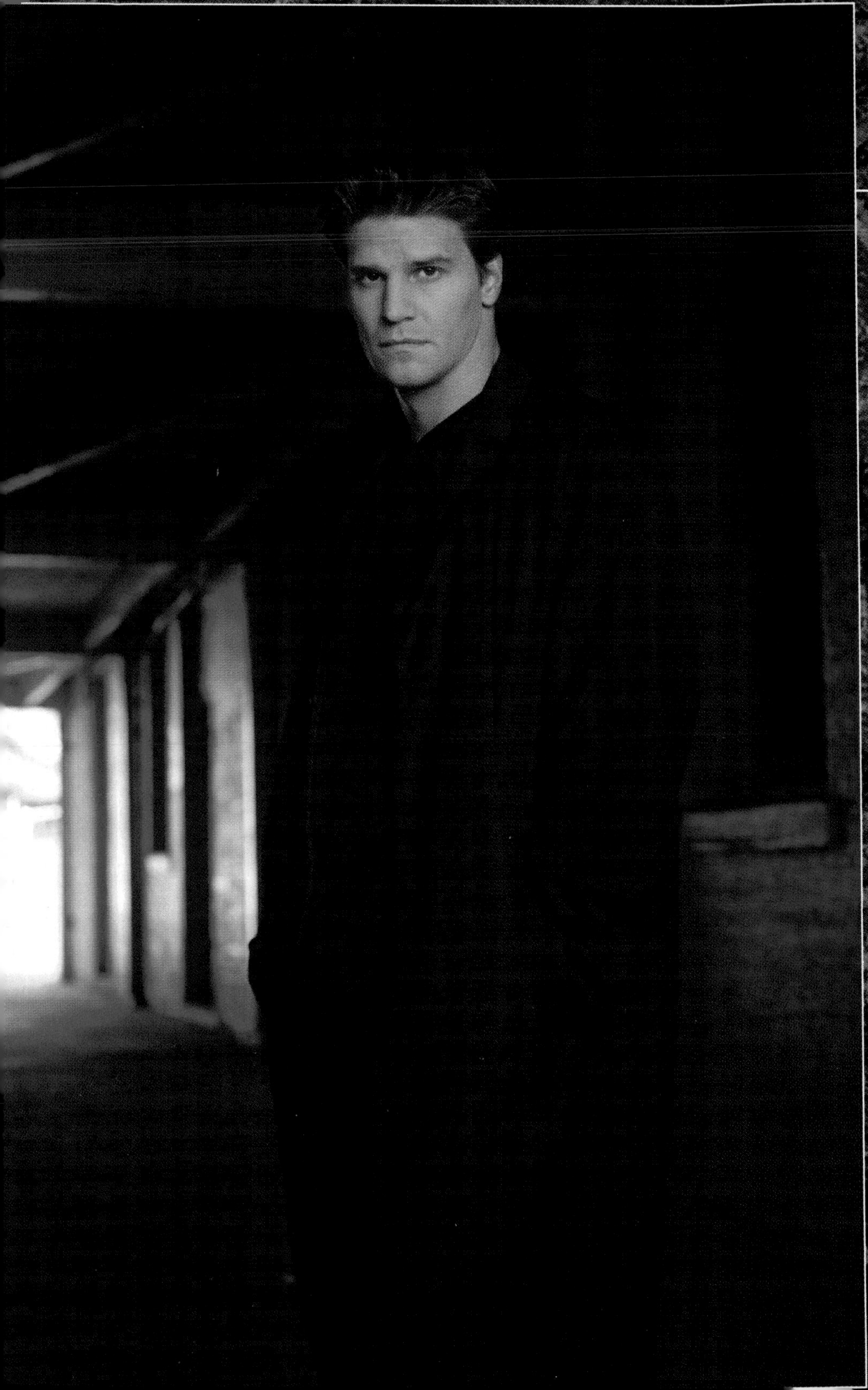

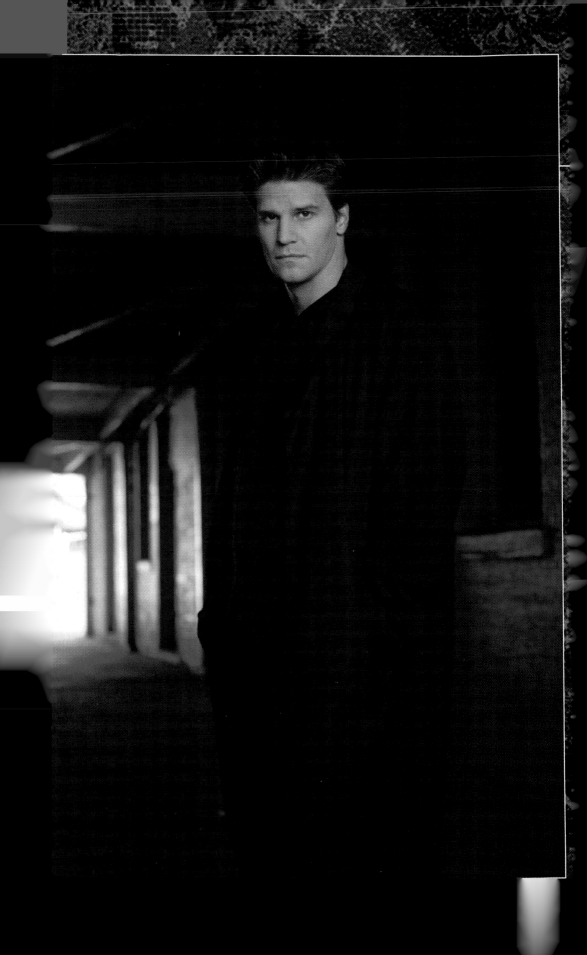

ANGEL™

Autumnal

based on the television series
created by
JOSS WHEDON and DAVID GREENWALT

by
CHRISTOPHER GOLDEN, TOM SNIEGOSKI,
CHRISTIAN ZANIER, and ERIC POWELL

with
MARVIN MARIANO, ANDREW PEPOY,
MARK HEIKE, CLAYTON BROWN,
CHRIS IVY, DEREK FRIDOLFS,
JASON MOORE, LEE LOUGHRIDGE,
CLEM ROBINS, and PAT BROSSEAU

DARK HORSE COMICS®

publisher
MIKE RICHARDSON

editor
SCOTT ALLIE
with ADAM GALLARDO and MIKE CARRIGLITTO

collection designers
KEITH WOOD and DARCY HOCKETT

art director
MARK COX

Special thanks to
DEBBIE OLSHAN at Fox Licensing,
CAROLINE KALLAS and GEORGE SNYDER at
Buffy the Vampire Slayer.

Published by
Dark Horse Comics, Inc.
10956 SE Main Street
Milwaukie, OR 97222

First edition: December 2001
ISBN: 1-56971-559-9

1 3 5 7 9 10 8 6 4 2

Printed in Singapore.
These stories take place during **Angel's** first season.

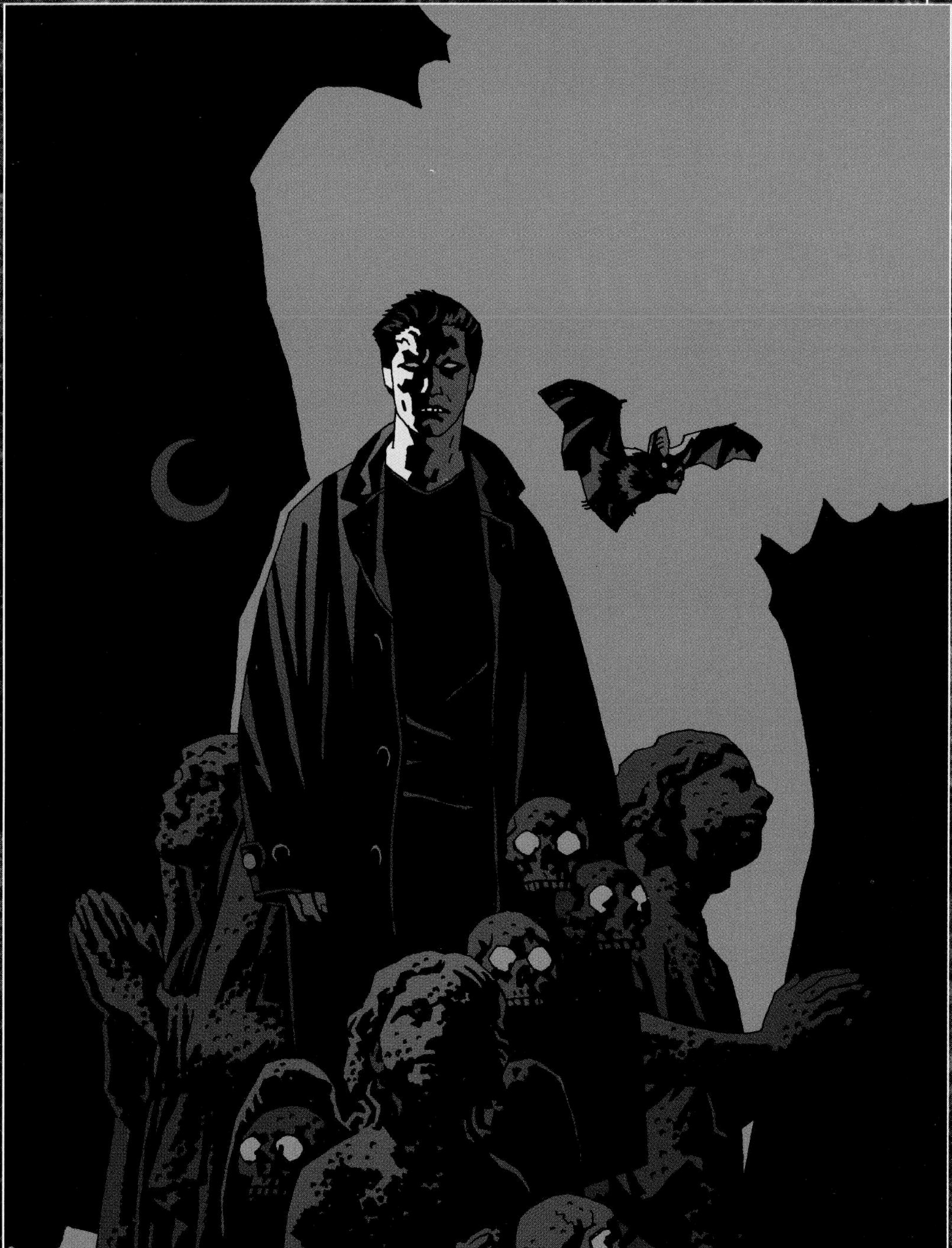
MIGNOLA
99

Art by MIKE MIGNOLA
with DAVE STEWART

Vermin

writers
CHRISTOPHER GOLDEN
and TOM SNIEGOSKI

penciller
CHRISTIAN ZANIER
with MARVIN MARIANO

inkers
ANDREW PEPOY,
MARK HEIKE,
CLAYTON BROWN,
CHRIS IVY
& DEREK FRIDOLFS

colorist
LEE LOUGHRIDGE

letterer
CLEM ROBINS

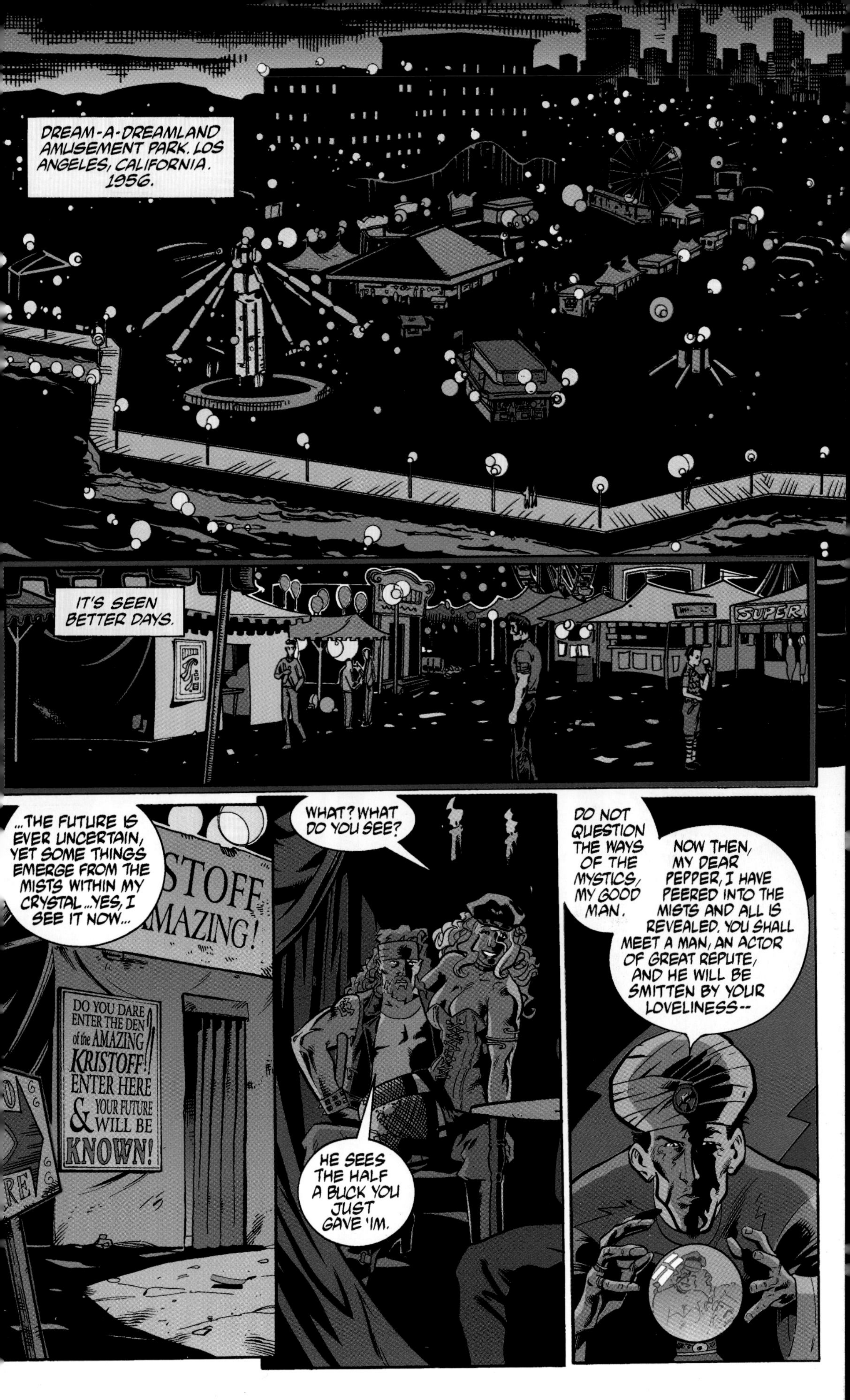
DREAM-A-DREAMLAND AMUSEMENT PARK. LOS ANGELES, CALIFORNIA. 1956.
IT'S SEEN BETTER DAYS.
SUPER
...THE FUTURE IS EVER UNCERTAIN, YET SOME THINGS EMERGE FROM THE MISTS WITHIN MY CRYSTAL...YES, I SEE IT NOW...
STOFF
AMAZING!
DO YOU DARE ENTER THE DEN of the AMAZING KRISTOFF!! ENTER HERE & YOUR FUTURE WILL BE KNOWN!
WHAT? WHAT DO YOU SEE?
HE SEES THE HALF A BUCK YOU JUST GAVE 'IM.
DO NOT QUESTION THE WAYS OF THE MYSTICS, MY GOOD MAN.
NOW THEN, MY DEAR PEPPER, I HAVE PEERED INTO THE MISTS AND ALL IS REVEALED. YOU SHALL MEET A MAN, AN ACTOR OF GREAT REPUTE, AND HE WILL BE SMITTEN BY YOUR LOVELINESS--

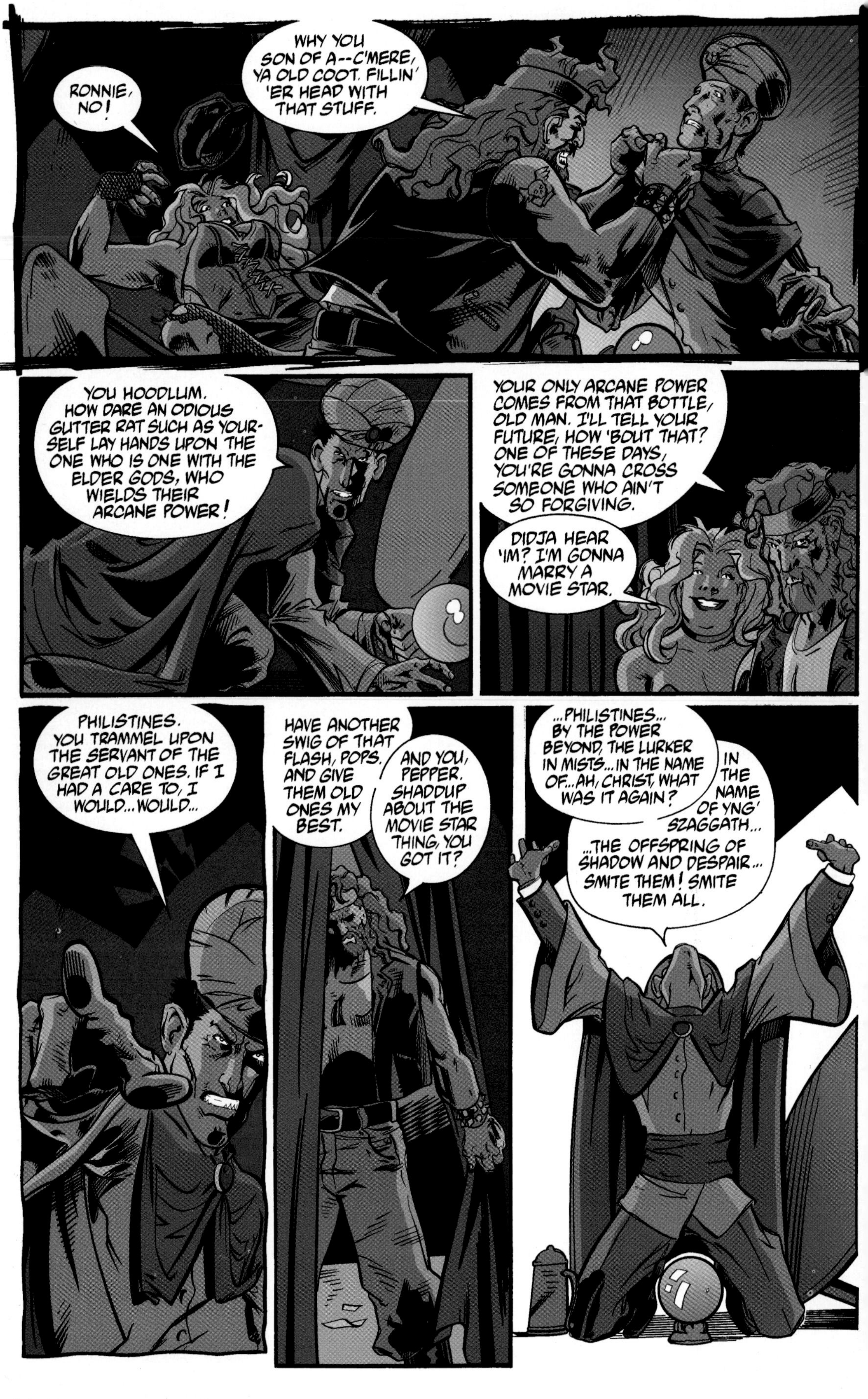
RONNIE, NO!
WHY YOU SON OF A--C'MERE, YA OLD COOT. FILLIN' 'ER HEAD WITH THAT STUFF.
YOU HOODLUM. HOW DARE AN ODIOUS GUTTER RAT SUCH AS YOURSELF LAY HANDS UPON THE ONE WHO IS ONE WITH THE ELDER GODS, WHO WIELDS THEIR ARCANE POWER!
YOUR ONLY ARCANE POWER COMES FROM THAT BOTTLE, OLD MAN. I'LL TELL YOUR FUTURE, HOW 'BOUT THAT? ONE OF THESE DAYS, YOU'RE GONNA CROSS SOMEONE WHO AIN'T SO FORGIVING.
DIDJA HEAR 'IM? I'M GONNA MARRY A MOVIE STAR.
PHILISTINES. YOU TRAMMEL UPON THE SERVANT OF THE GREAT OLD ONES. IF I HAD A CARE TO, I WOULD...WOULD...
HAVE ANOTHER SWIG OF THAT FLASH, POPS, AND GIVE THEM OLD ONES MY BEST.
AND YOU, PEPPER. SHADDUP ABOUT THE MOVIE STAR THING, YOU GOT IT?
...PHILISTINES... BY THE POWER BEYOND, THE LURKER IN MISTS...IN THE NAME OF...AH, CHRIST, WHAT WAS IT AGAIN?
IN THE NAME OF YNG' SZAGGATH...
...THE OFFSPRING OF SHADOW AND DESPAIR... SMITE THEM! SMITE THEM ALL.

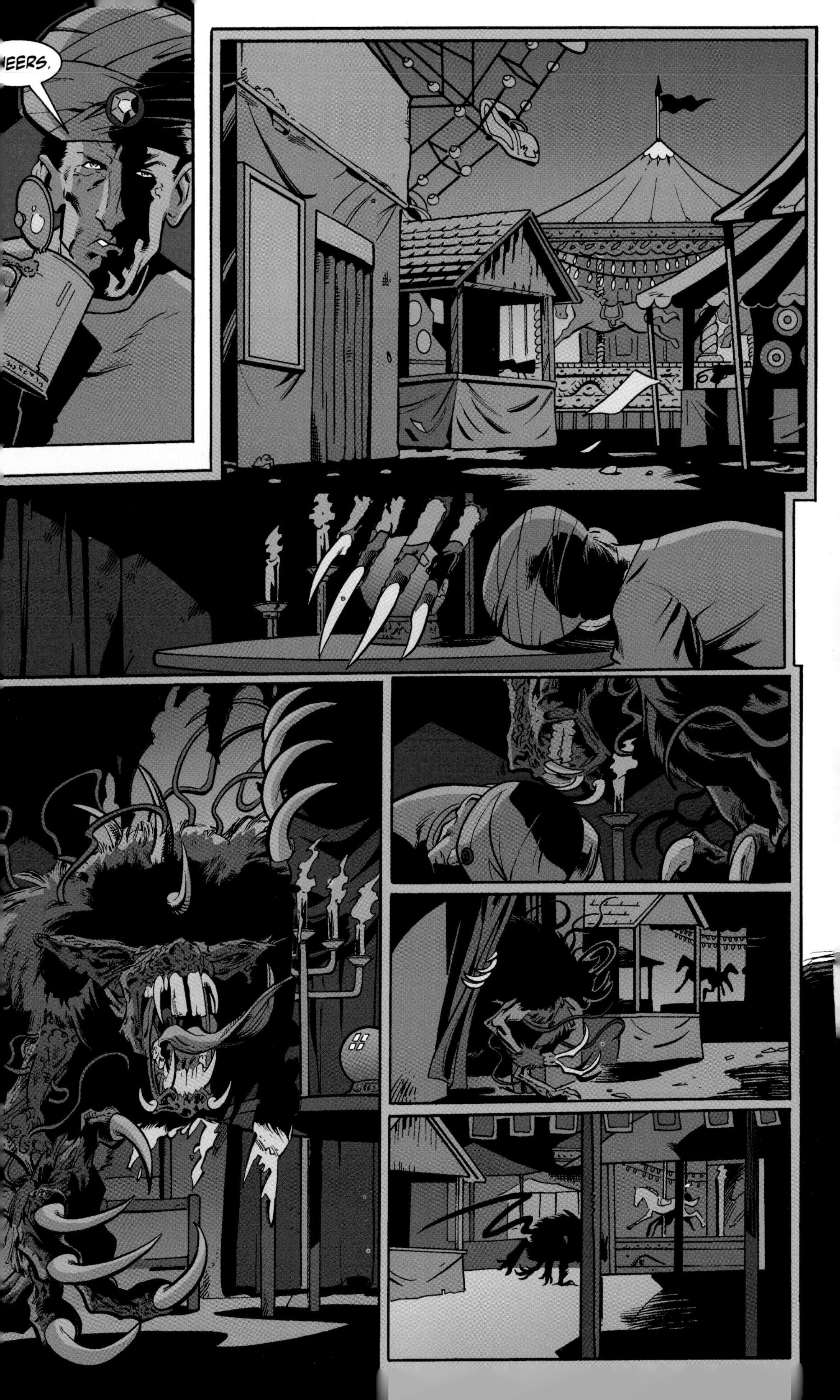
EERS.

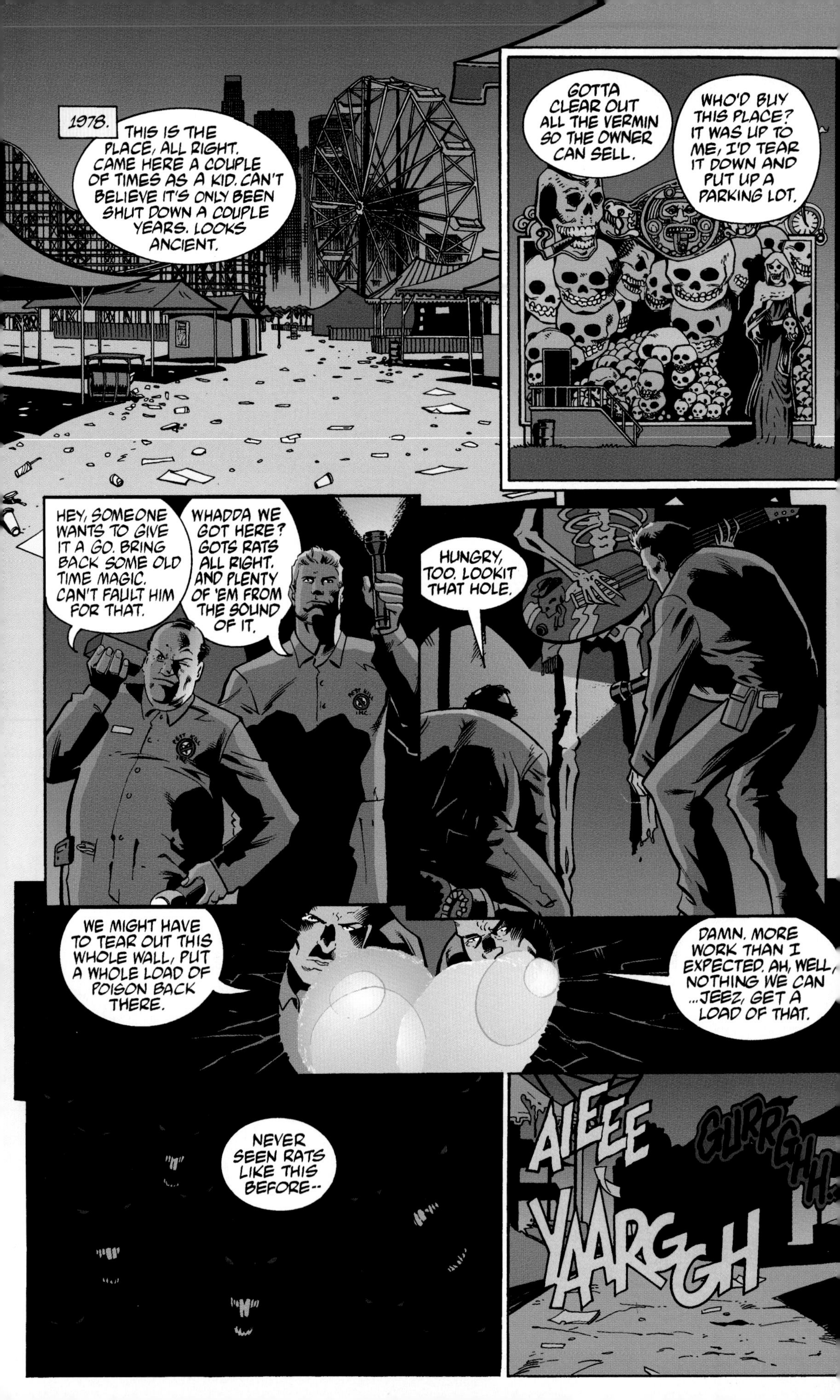
1978.
THIS IS THE PLACE, ALL RIGHT. CAME HERE A COUPLE OF TIMES AS A KID. CAN'T BELIEVE IT'S ONLY BEEN SHUT DOWN A COUPLE YEARS. LOOKS ANCIENT.
GOTTA CLEAR OUT ALL THE VERMIN SO THE OWNER CAN SELL.
WHO'D BUY THIS PLACE? IT WAS UP TO ME, I'D TEAR IT DOWN AND PUT UP A PARKING LOT.
HEY, SOMEONE WANTS TO GIVE IT A GO. BRING BACK SOME OLD TIME MAGIC. CAN'T FAULT HIM FOR THAT.
WHADDA WE GOT HERE? GOTS RATS ALL RIGHT. AND PLENTY OF 'EM FROM THE SOUND OF IT.
HUNGRY, TOO. LOOKIT THAT HOLE.
WE MIGHT HAVE TO TEAR OUT THIS WHOLE WALL, PUT A WHOLE LOAD OF POISON BACK THERE.
DAMN. MORE WORK THAN I EXPECTED. AH, WELL, NOTHING WE CAN ...JEEZ, GET A LOAD OF THAT.
NEVER SEEN RATS LIKE THIS BEFORE--
AIEEE
GURRGHH
YAARGGH

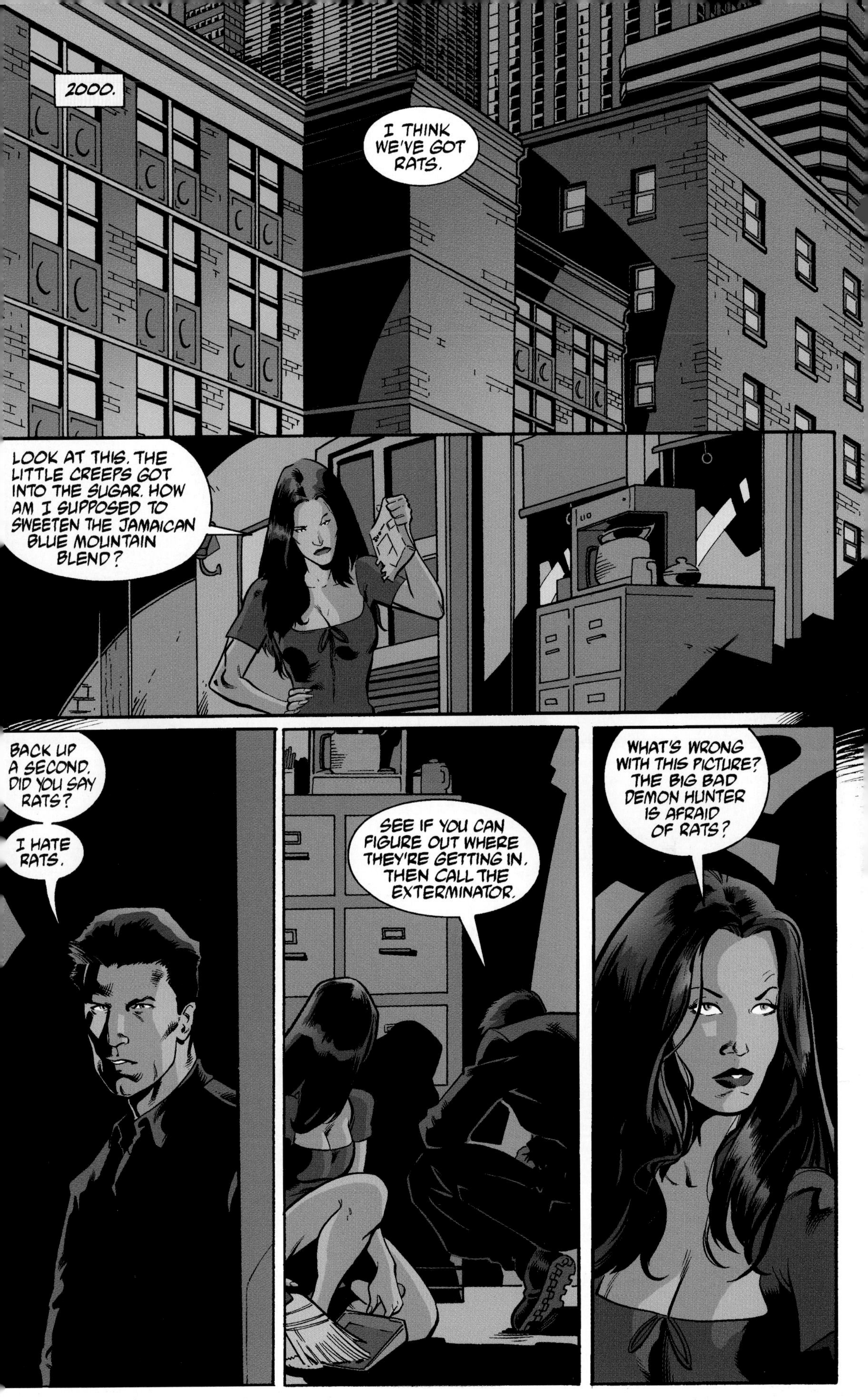
2000.
I THINK WE'VE GOT RATS.
LOOK AT THIS. THE LITTLE CREEPS GOT INTO THE SUGAR. HOW AM I SUPPOSED TO SWEETEN THE JAMAICAN BLUE MOUNTAIN BLEND?
BACK UP A SECOND. DID YOU SAY RATS?
I HATE RATS.
SEE IF YOU CAN FIGURE OUT WHERE THEY'RE GETTING IN, THEN CALL THE EXTERMINATOR.
WHAT'S WRONG WITH THIS PICTURE? THE BIG BAD DEMON HUNTER IS AFRAID OF RATS?

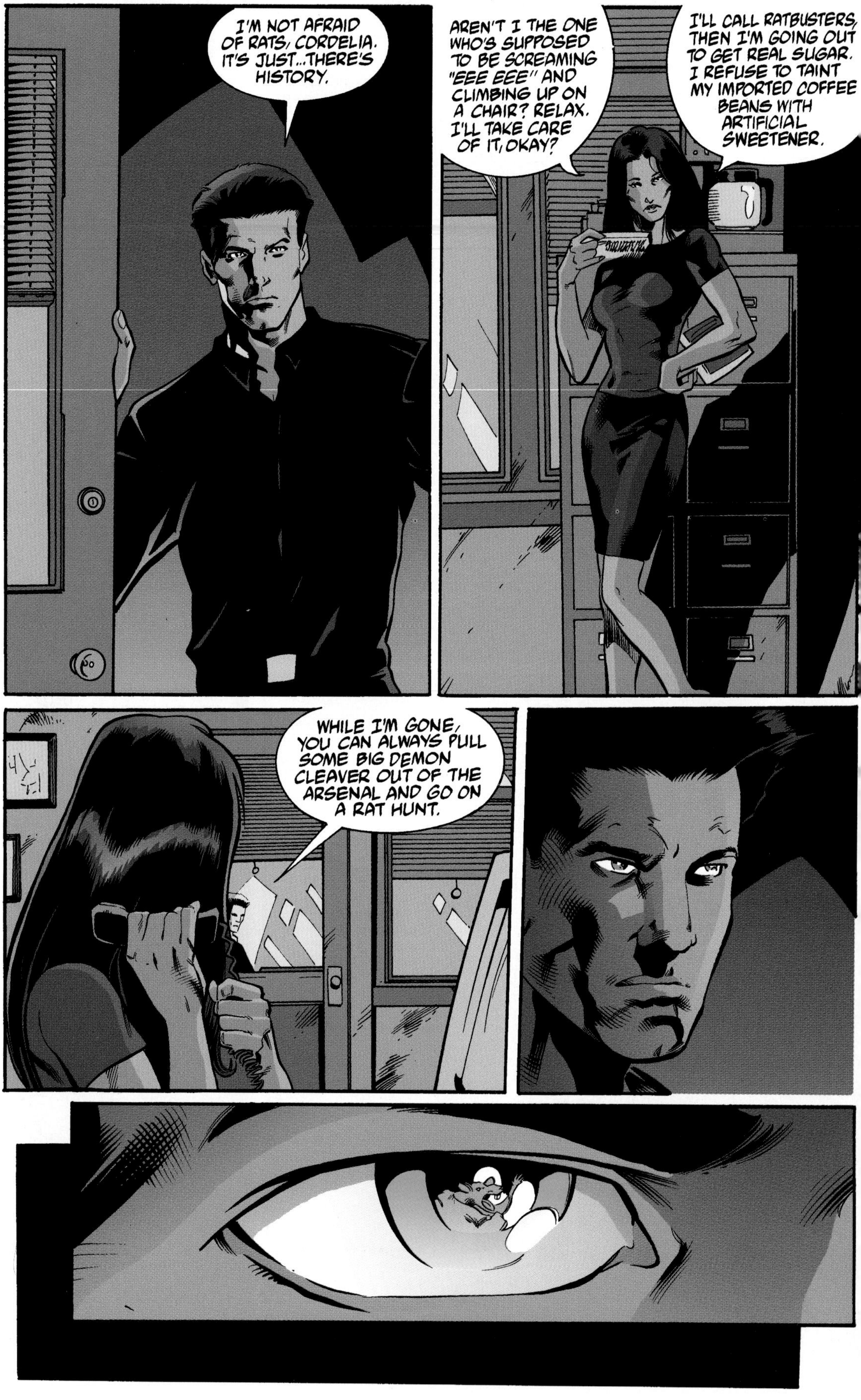
I'M NOT AFRAID OF RATS, CORDELIA. IT'S JUST...THERE'S HISTORY.
AREN'T I THE ONE WHO'S SUPPOSED TO BE SCREAMING "EEE EEE" AND CLIMBING UP ON A CHAIR? RELAX. I'LL TAKE CARE OF IT, OKAY?
I'LL CALL RATBUSTERS, THEN I'M GOING OUT TO GET REAL SUGAR. I REFUSE TO TAINT MY IMPORTED COFFEE BEANS WITH ARTIFICIAL SWEETENER.
WHILE I'M GONE, YOU CAN ALWAYS PULL SOME BIG DEMON CLEAVER OUT OF THE ARSENAL AND GO ON A RAT HUNT.

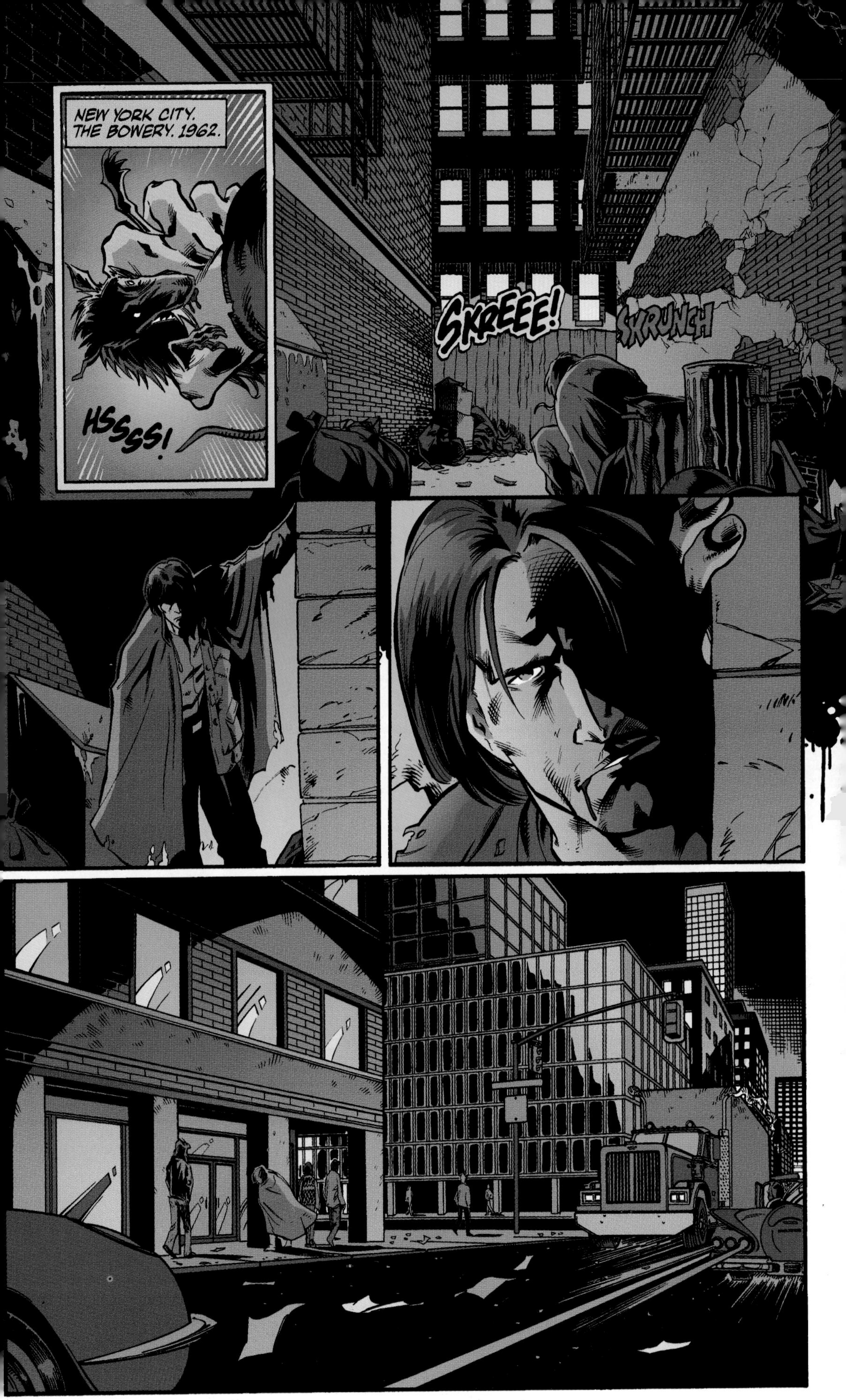
NEW YORK CITY.
THE BOWERY. 1962.
HSSSSS!
SKREEE!
SKRUNCH

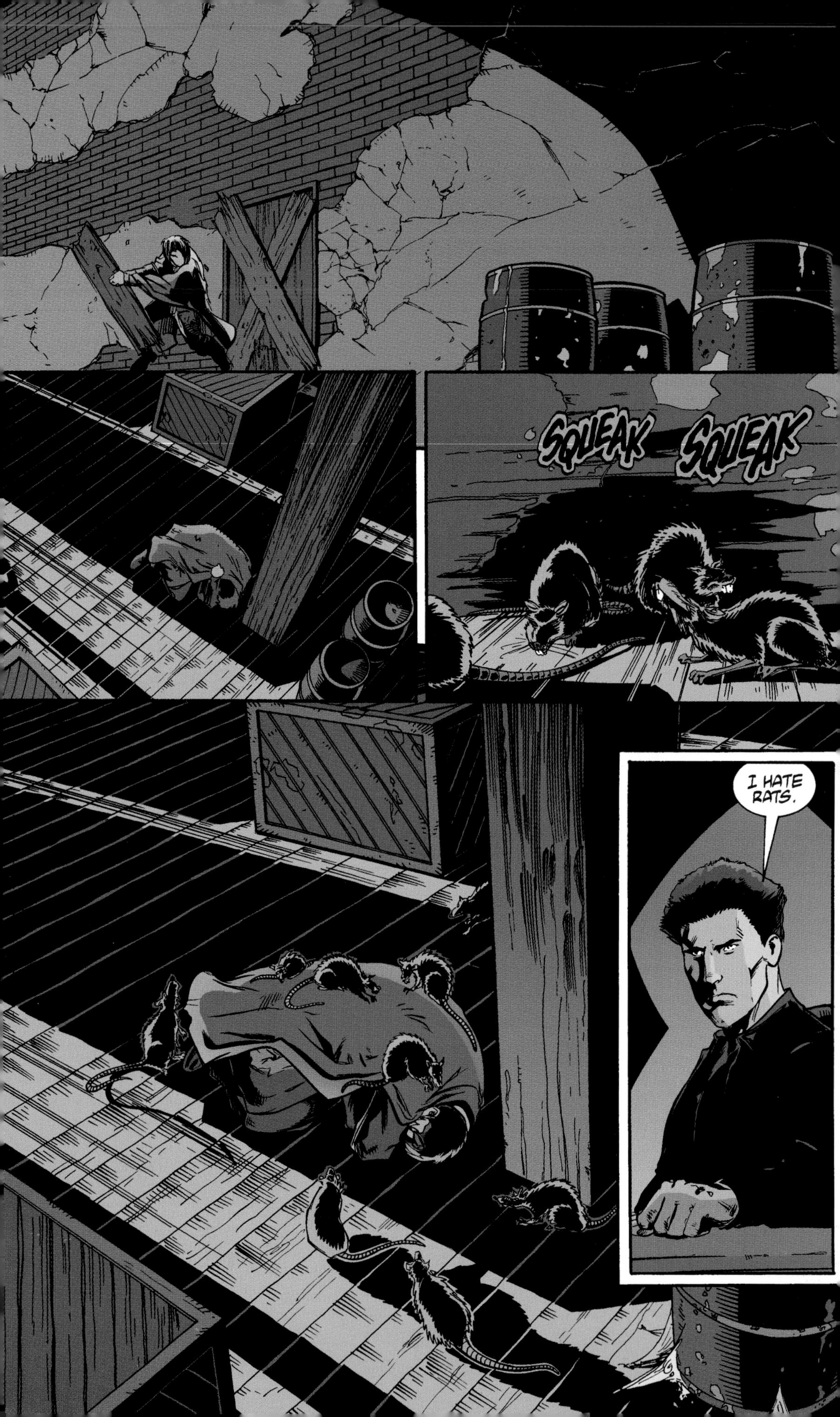
SQUEAK SQUEAK
I HATE RATS.

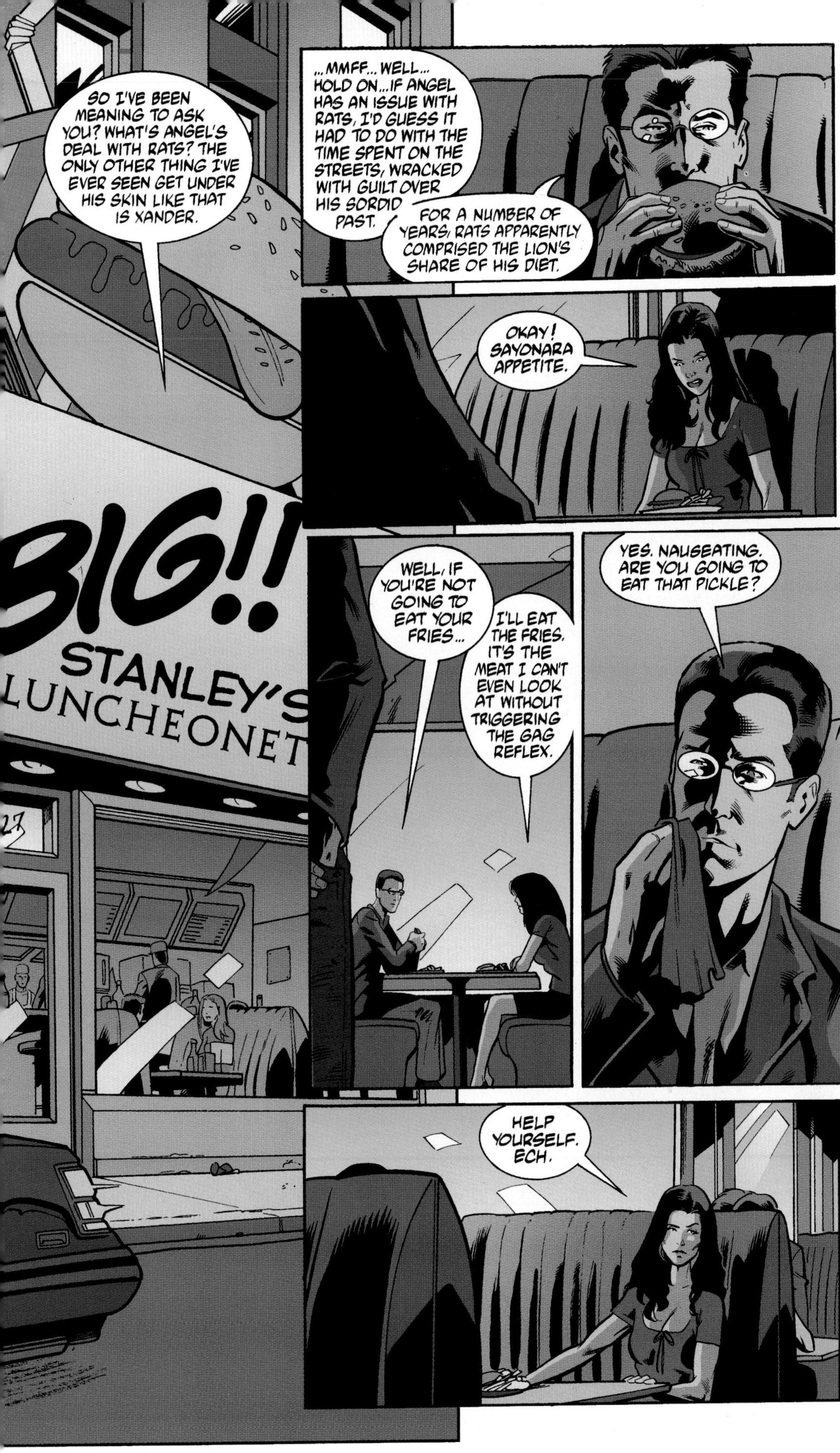
SO I'VE BEEN MEANING TO ASK YOU? WHAT'S ANGEL'S DEAL WITH RATS? THE ONLY OTHER THING I'VE EVER SEEN GET UNDER HIS SKIN LIKE THAT IS XANDER.
...MMFF... WELL... HOLD ON...IF ANGEL HAS AN ISSUE WITH RATS, I'D GUESS IT HAD TO DO WITH THE TIME SPENT ON THE STREETS, WRACKED WITH GUILT OVER HIS SORDID PAST.
FOR A NUMBER OF YEARS, RATS APPARENTLY COMPRISED THE LION'S SHARE OF HIS DIET.
OKAY! SAYONARA APPETITE.
BIG!!
STANLEY'S
LUNCHEONET
27
WELL, IF YOU'RE NOT GOING TO EAT YOUR FRIES...
I'LL EAT THE FRIES. IT'S THE MEAT I CAN'T EVEN LOOK AT WITHOUT TRIGGERING THE GAG REFLEX.
YES. NAUSEATING. ARE YOU GOING TO EAT THAT PICKLE?
HELP YOURSELF. ECH.

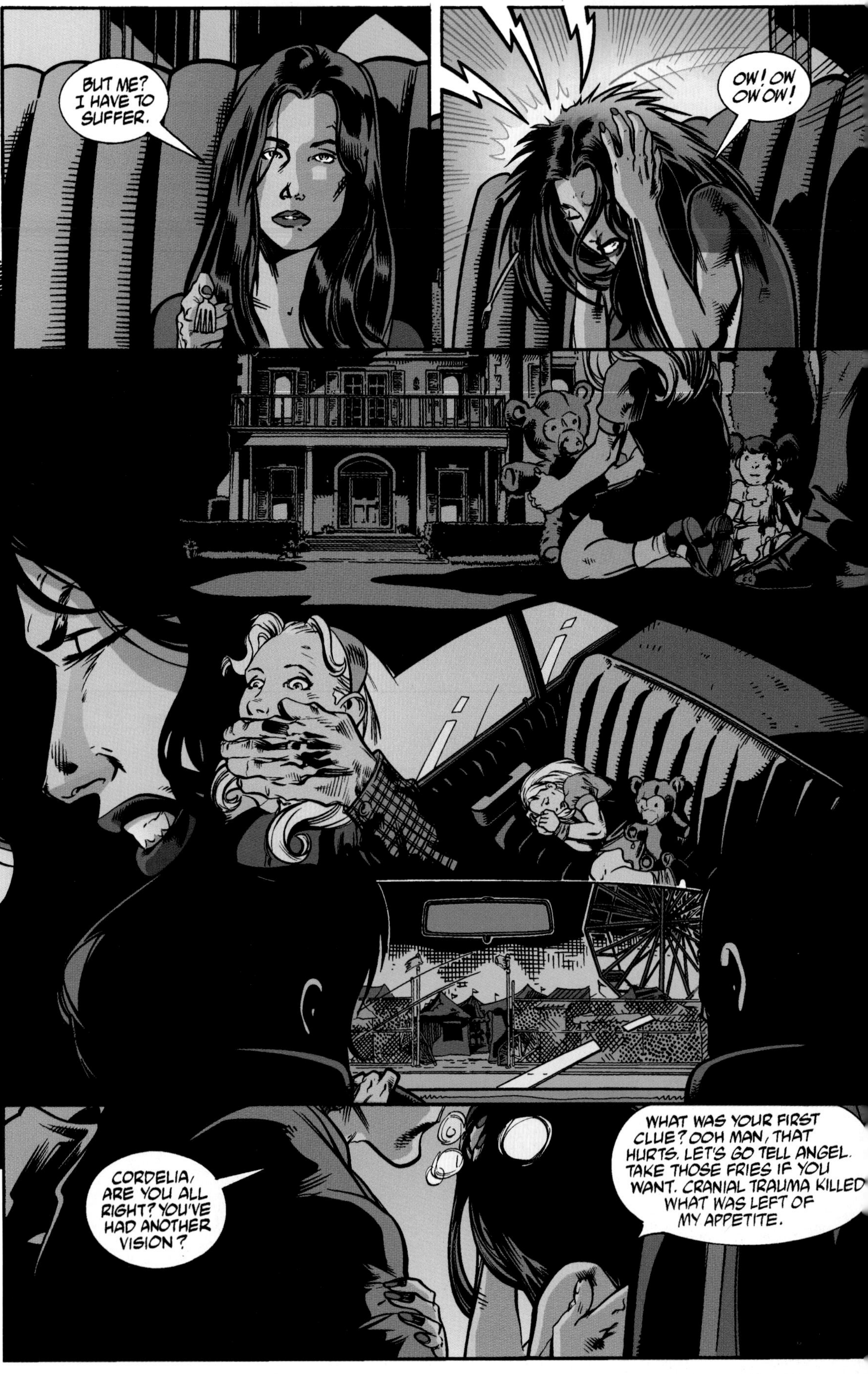
BUT ME? I HAVE TO SUFFER.
OW! OW OW OW!
CORDELIA, ARE YOU ALL RIGHT? YOU'VE HAD ANOTHER VISION?
WHAT WAS YOUR FIRST CLUE? OOH MAN, THAT HURTS. LET'S GO TELL ANGEL. TAKE THOSE FRIES IF YOU WANT. CRANIAL TRAUMA KILLED WHAT WAS LEFT OF MY APPETITE.

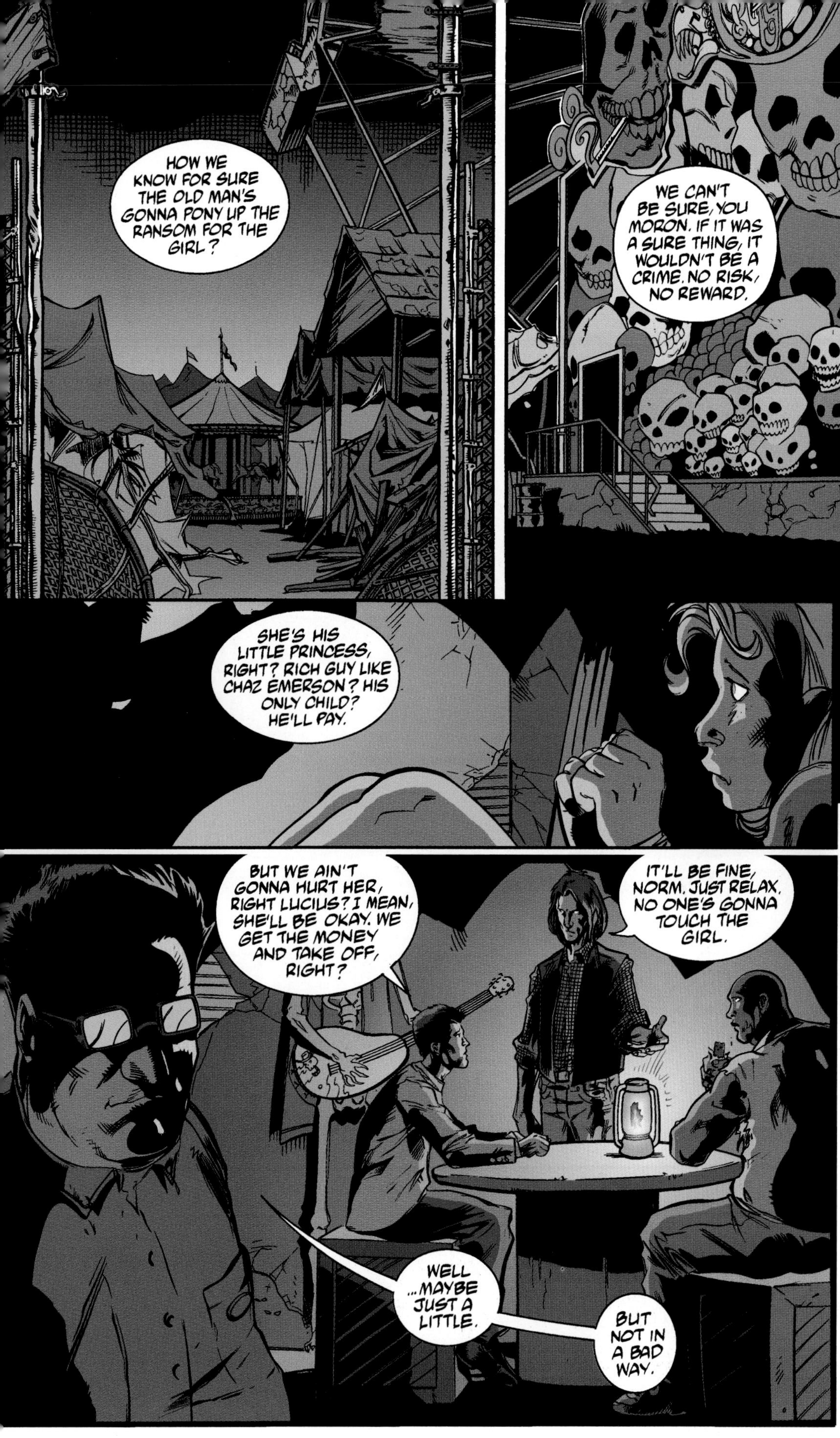
HOW WE KNOW FOR SURE THE OLD MAN'S GONNA PONY UP THE RANSOM FOR THE GIRL?
WE CAN'T BE SURE, YOU MORON. IF IT WAS A SURE THING, IT WOULDN'T BE A CRIME. NO RISK, NO REWARD.
SHE'S HIS LITTLE PRINCESS, RIGHT? RICH GUY LIKE CHAZ EMERSON? HIS ONLY CHILD? HE'LL PAY.
BUT WE AIN'T GONNA HURT HER, RIGHT LUCIUS? I MEAN, SHE'LL BE OKAY. WE GET THE MONEY AND TAKE OFF, RIGHT?
IT'LL BE FINE, NORM. JUST RELAX. NO ONE'S GONNA TOUCH THE GIRL.
WELL ...MAYBE JUST A LITTLE.
BUT NOT IN A BAD WAY.

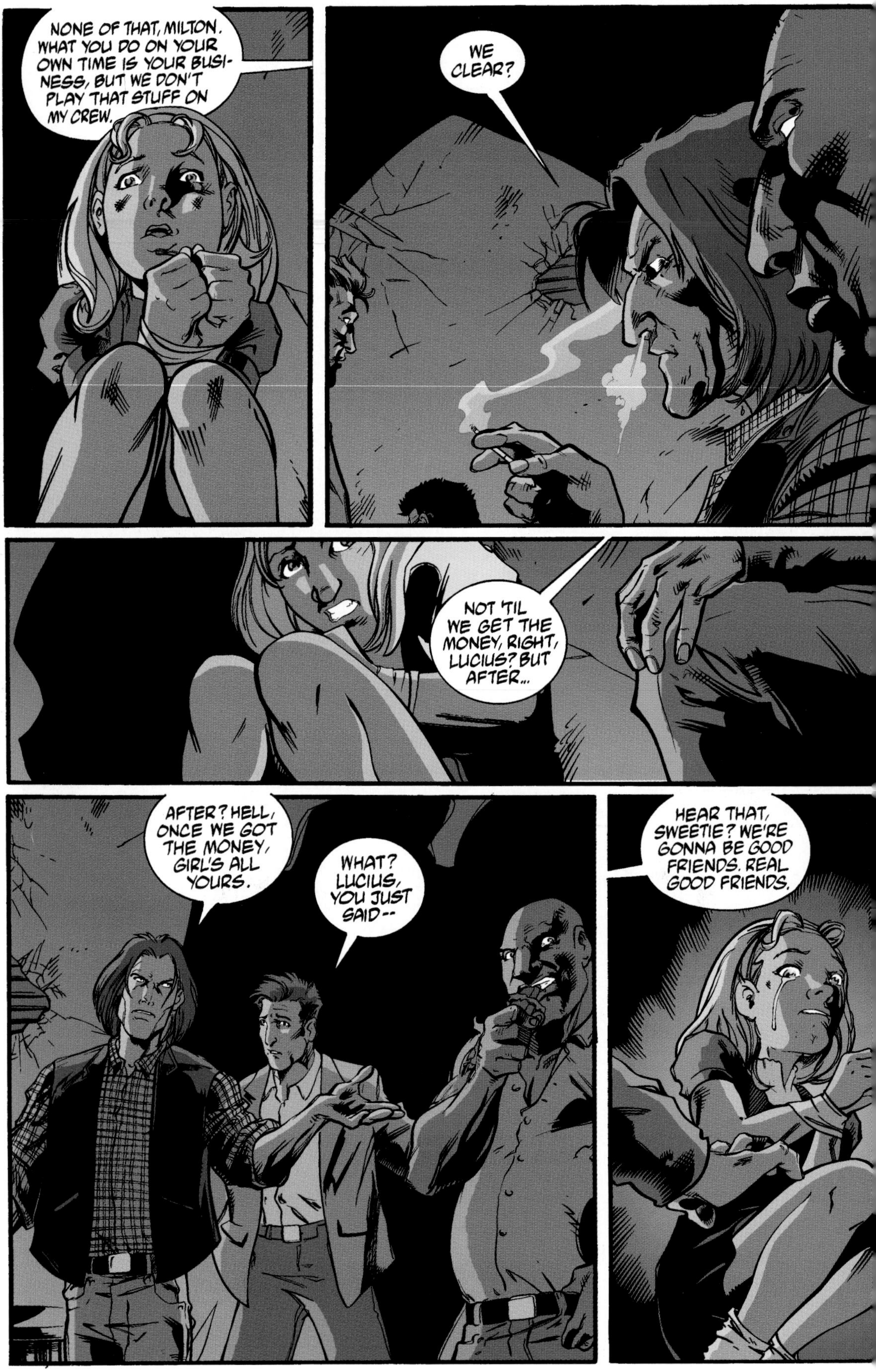
NONE OF THAT, MILTON. WHAT YOU DO ON YOUR OWN TIME IS YOUR BUSINESS, BUT WE DON'T PLAY THAT STUFF ON MY CREW.
WE CLEAR?
NOT 'TIL WE GET THE MONEY, RIGHT, LUCIUS? BUT AFTER...
AFTER? HELL, ONCE WE GOT THE MONEY, GIRL'S ALL YOURS.
WHAT? LUCIUS, YOU JUST SAID--
HEAR THAT, SWEETIE? WE'RE GONNA BE GOOD FRIENDS. REAL GOOD FRIENDS.

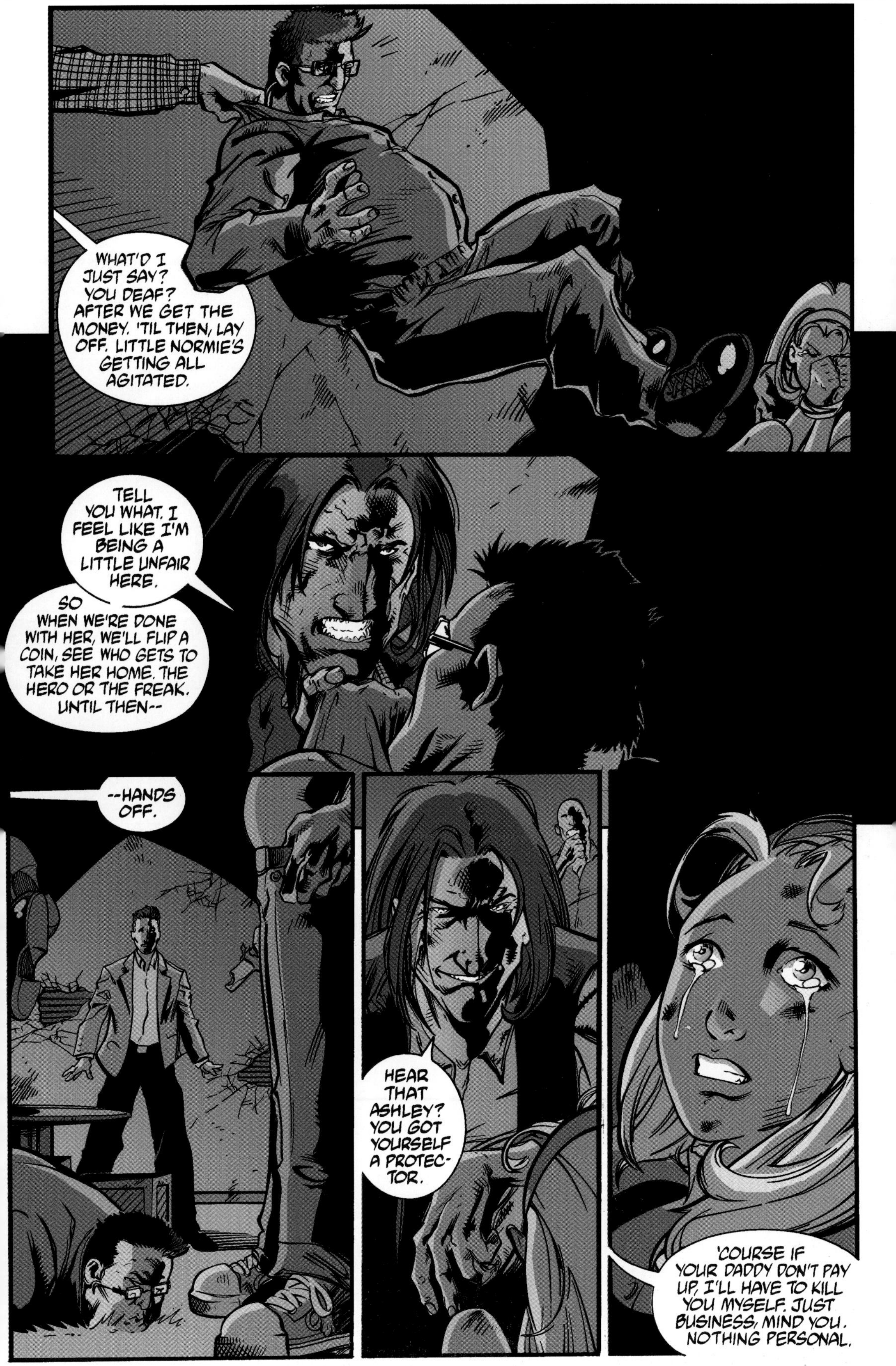
WHAT'D I JUST SAY? YOU DEAF? AFTER WE GET THE MONEY. 'TIL THEN, LAY OFF. LITTLE NORMIE'S GETTING ALL AGITATED.
TELL YOU WHAT. I FEEL LIKE I'M BEING A LITTLE UNFAIR HERE.
SO WHEN WE'RE DONE WITH HER, WE'LL FLIP A COIN, SEE WHO GETS TO TAKE HER HOME. THE HERO OR THE FREAK. UNTIL THEN--
--HANDS OFF.
HEAR THAT ASHLEY? YOU GOT YOURSELF A PROTEC-TOR.
'COURSE IF YOUR DADDY DON'T PAY UP, I'LL HAVE TO KILL YOU MYSELF. JUST BUSINESS, MIND YOU. NOTHING PERSONAL.

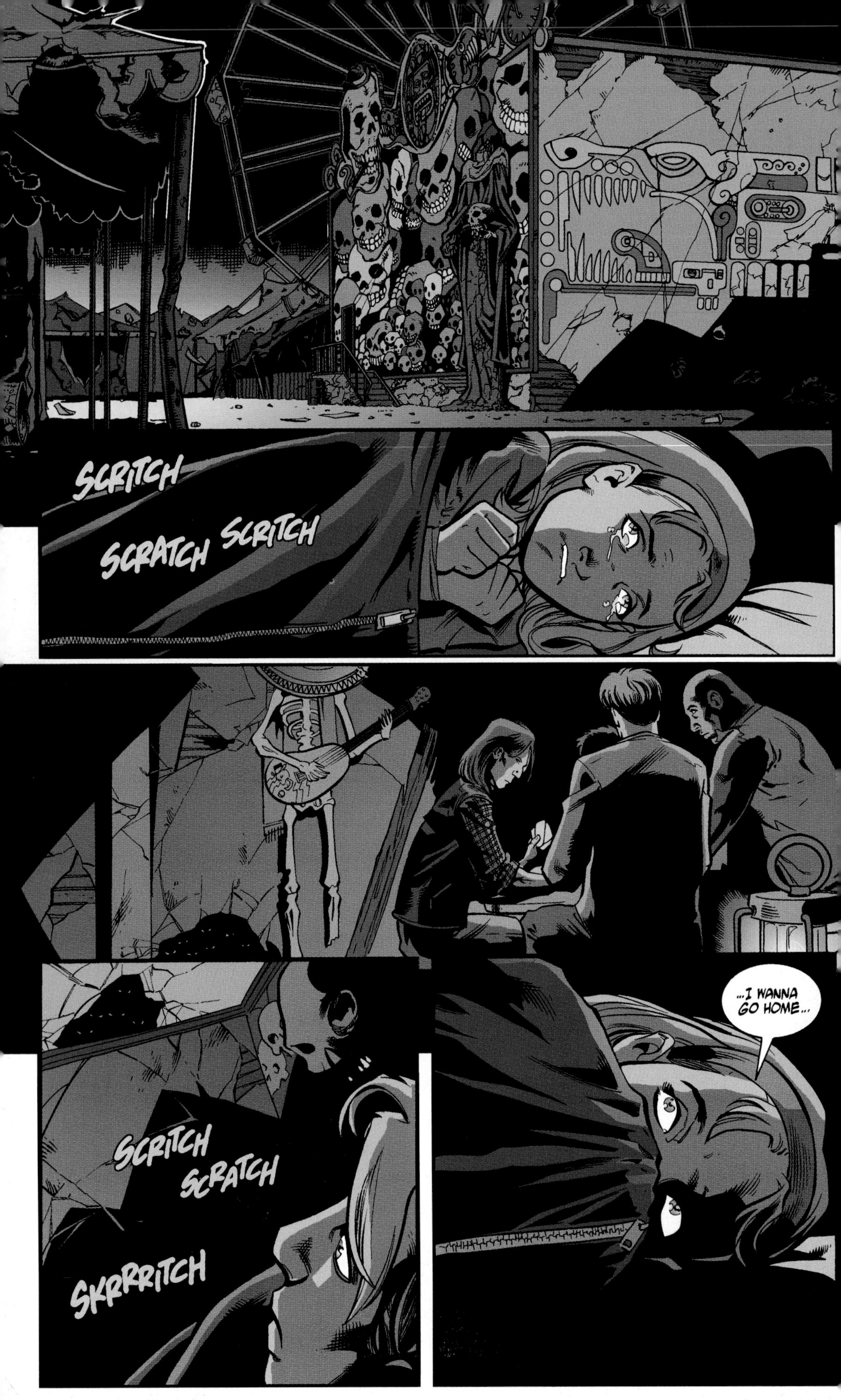
SCRITCH
SCRATCH SCRITCH
SCRITCH
SCRATCH
SKRRRITCH
...I WANNA GO HOME...

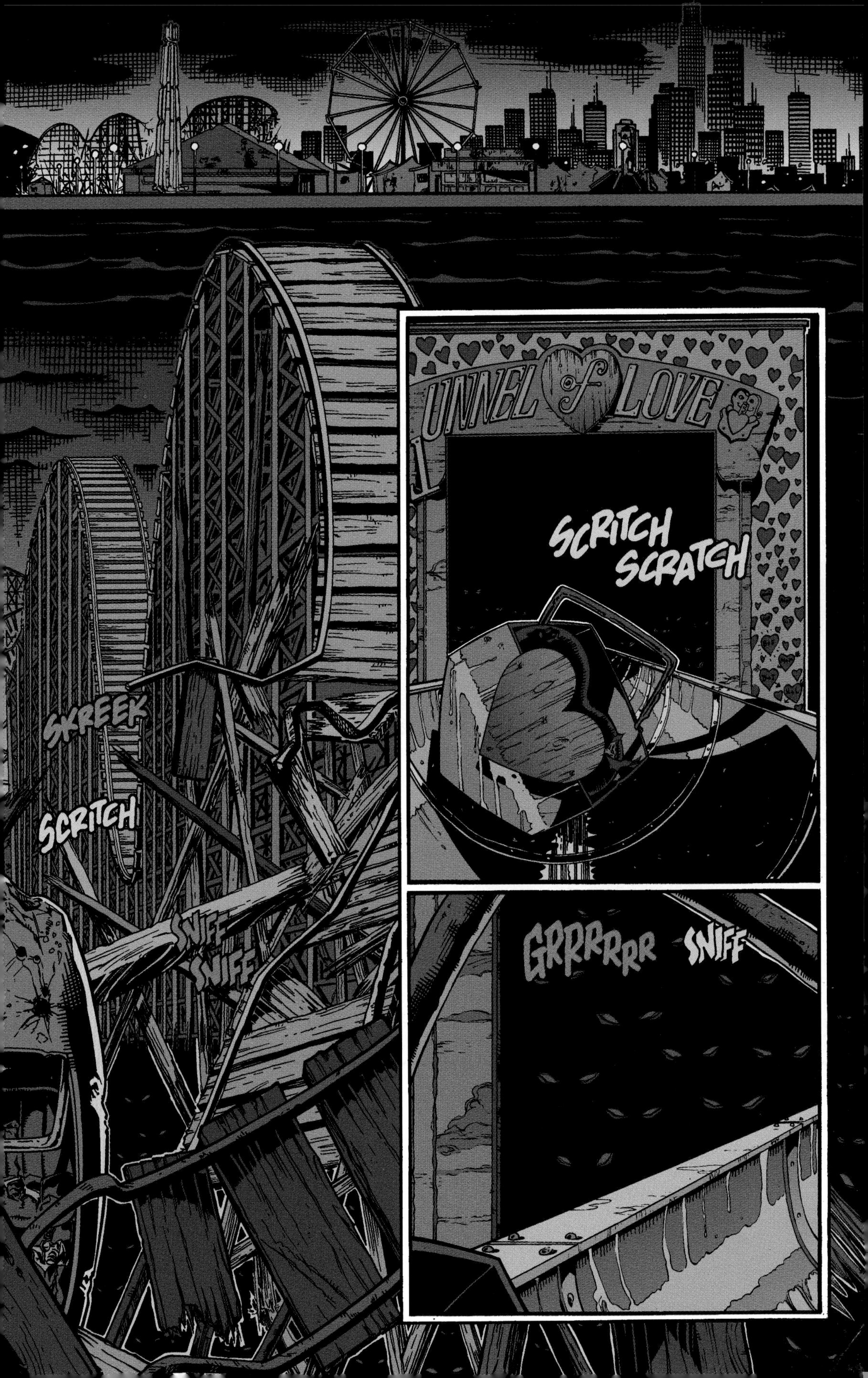

SKREEK
SCRITCH
SNIFF SNIFF
UNNEL of LOVE
SCRITCH SCRATCH
GRRRRRR
SNIFF

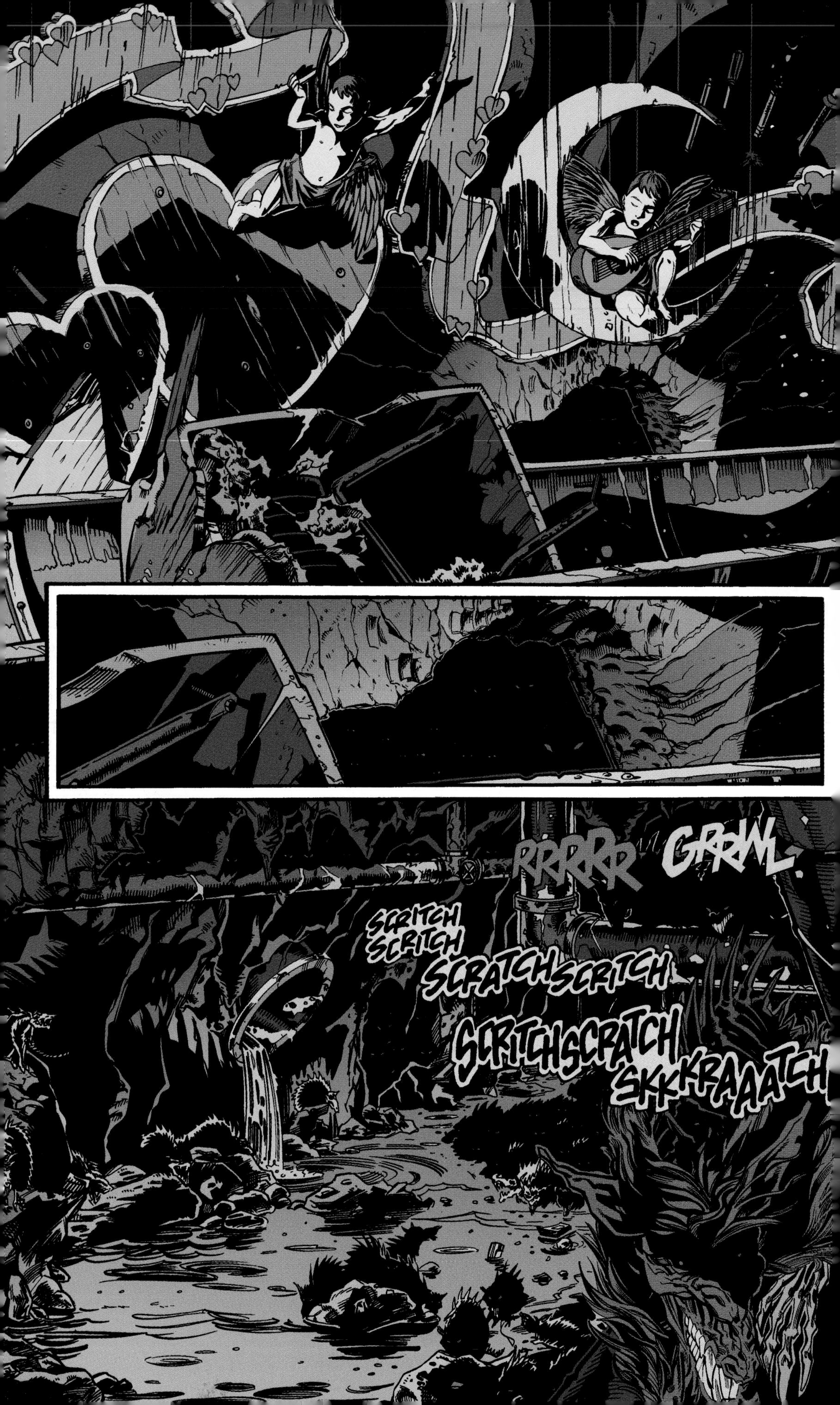
RRRRR GRRWL
SCRITCH SCRITCH
SCRATCHSCRITCH
SCRITCHSCRATCH
SKKRAAATCH

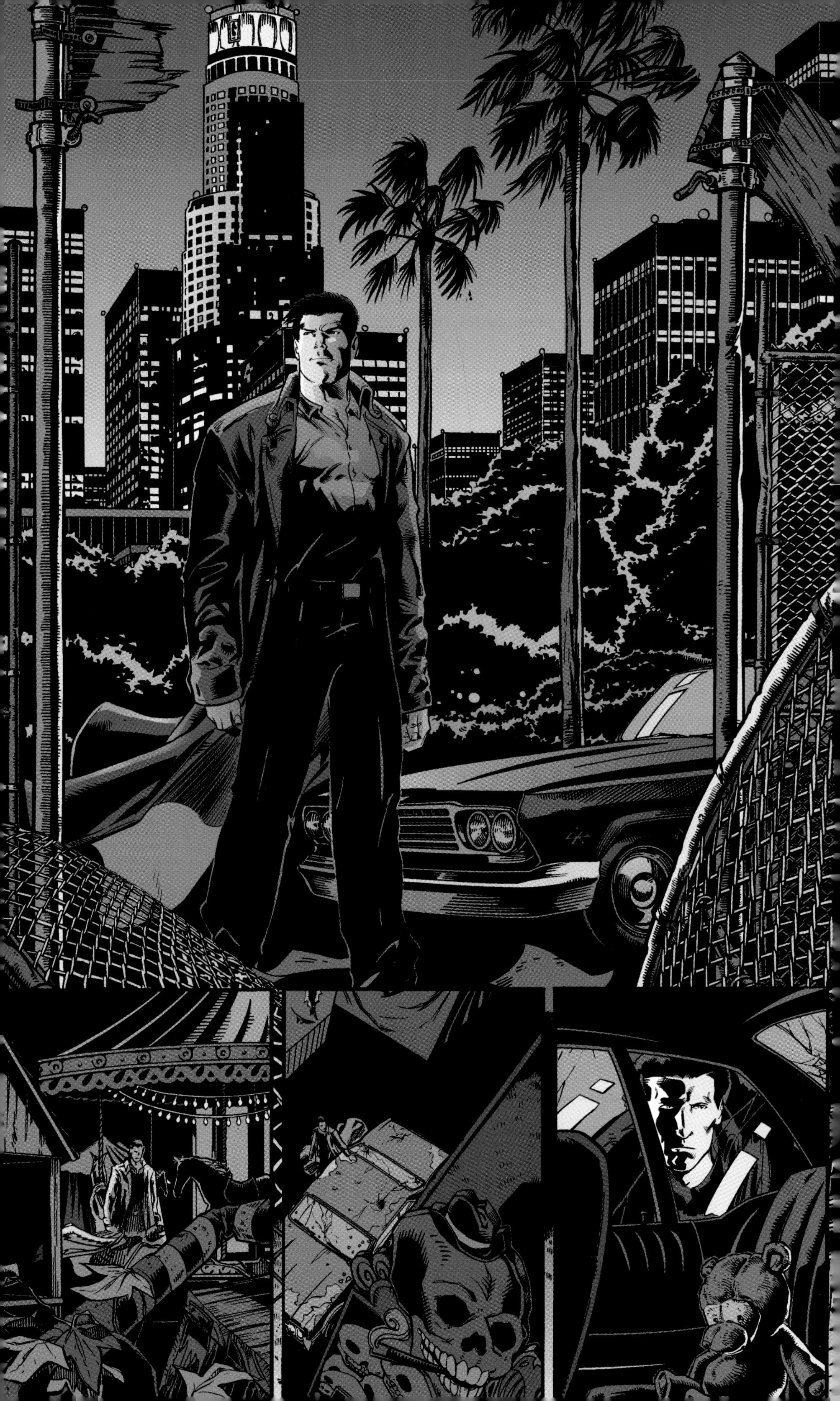

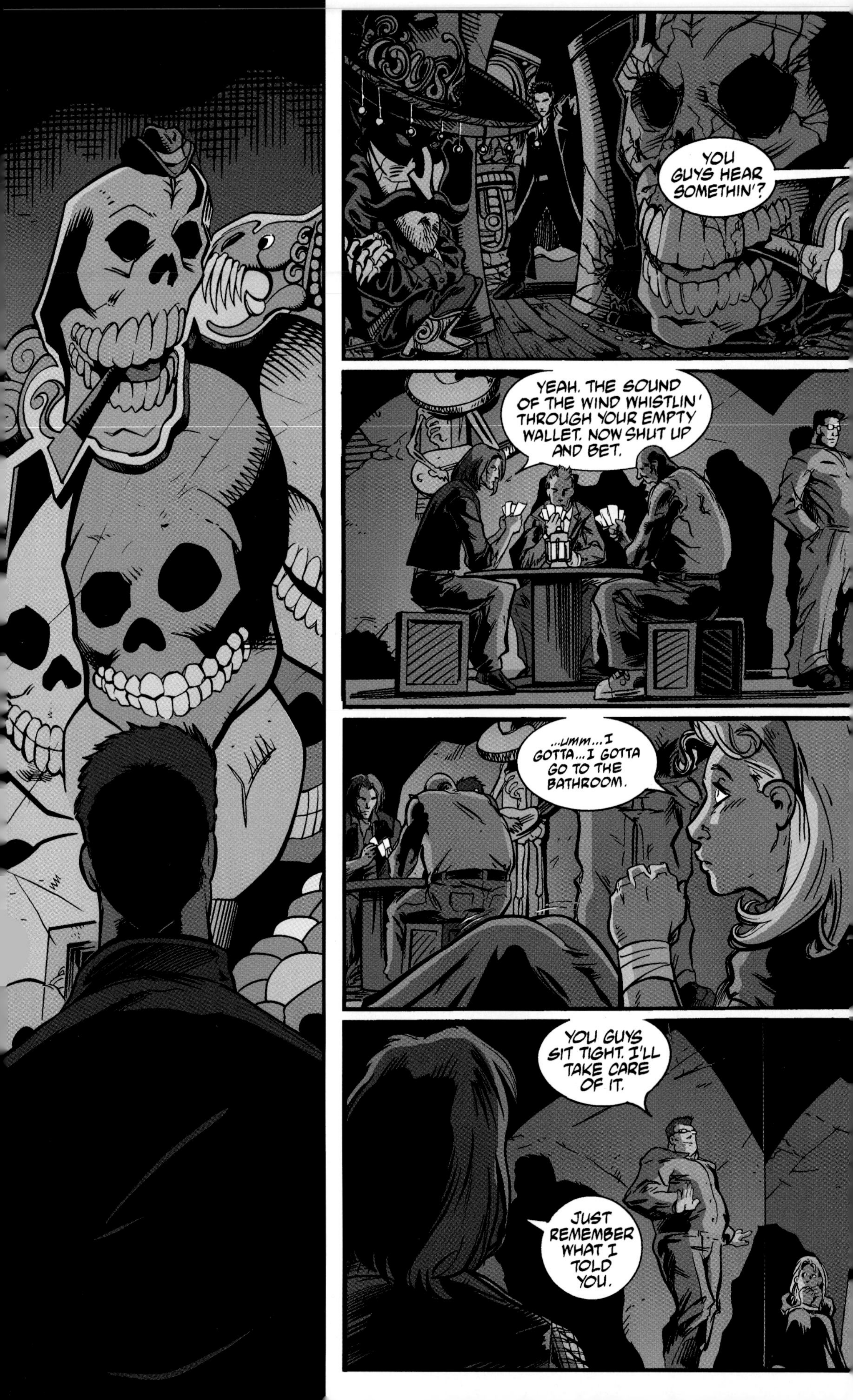
YOU GUYS HEAR SOMETHIN'?
YEAH. THE SOUND OF THE WIND WHISTLIN' THROUGH YOUR EMPTY WALLET. NOW SHUT UP AND BET.
...UMM... I GOTTA... I GOTTA GO TO THE BATHROOM.
YOU GUYS SIT TIGHT. I'LL TAKE CARE OF IT.
JUST REMEMBER WHAT I TOLD YOU.

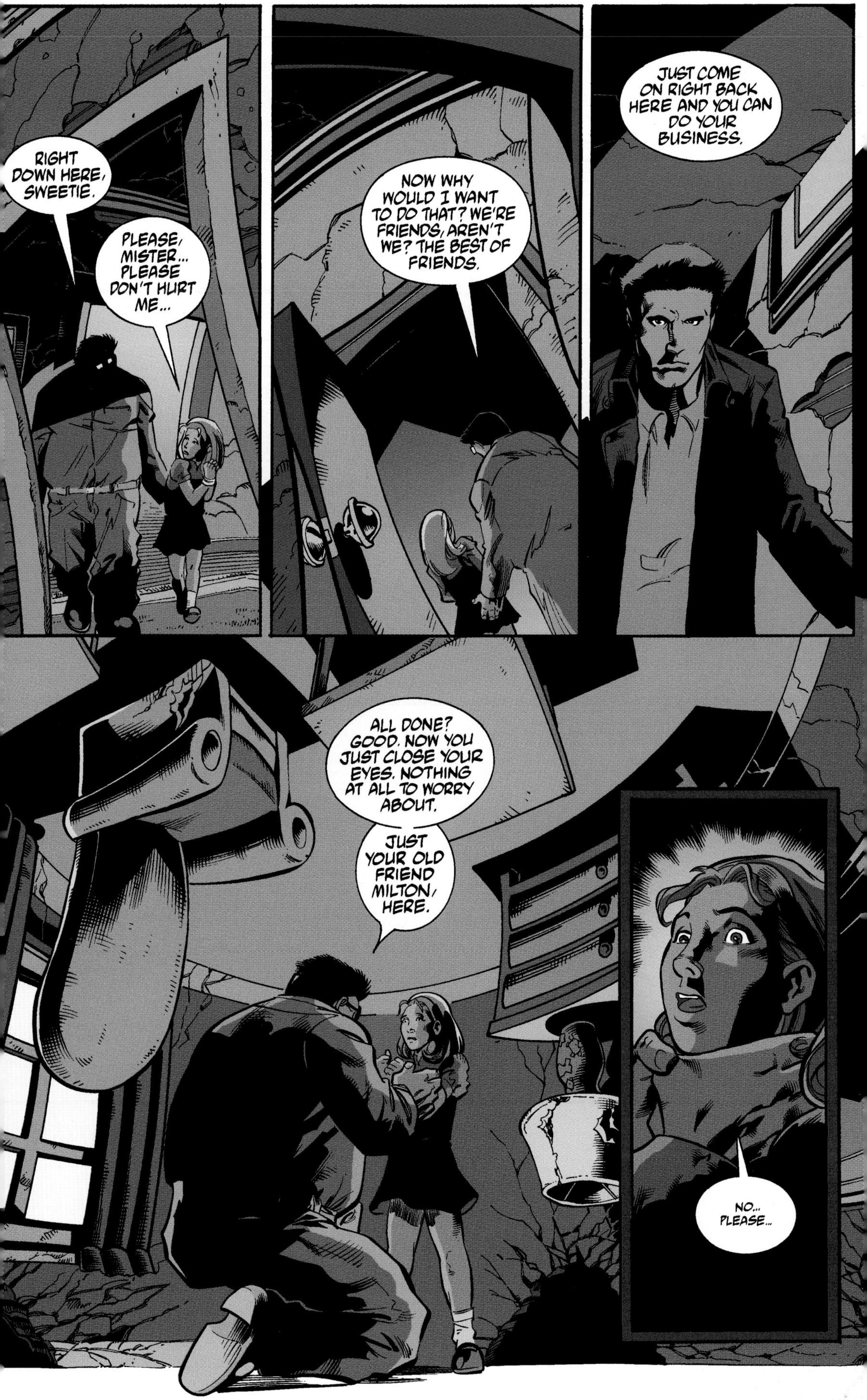
RIGHT DOWN HERE, SWEETIE.
PLEASE, MISTER... PLEASE DON'T HURT ME...
NOW WHY WOULD I WANT TO DO THAT? WE'RE FRIENDS, AREN'T WE? THE BEST OF FRIENDS.
JUST COME ON RIGHT BACK HERE AND YOU CAN DO YOUR BUSINESS.
ALL DONE? GOOD. NOW YOU JUST CLOSE YOUR EYES. NOTHING AT ALL TO WORRY ABOUT.
JUST YOUR OLD FRIEND MILTON, HERE.
NO... PLEASE...

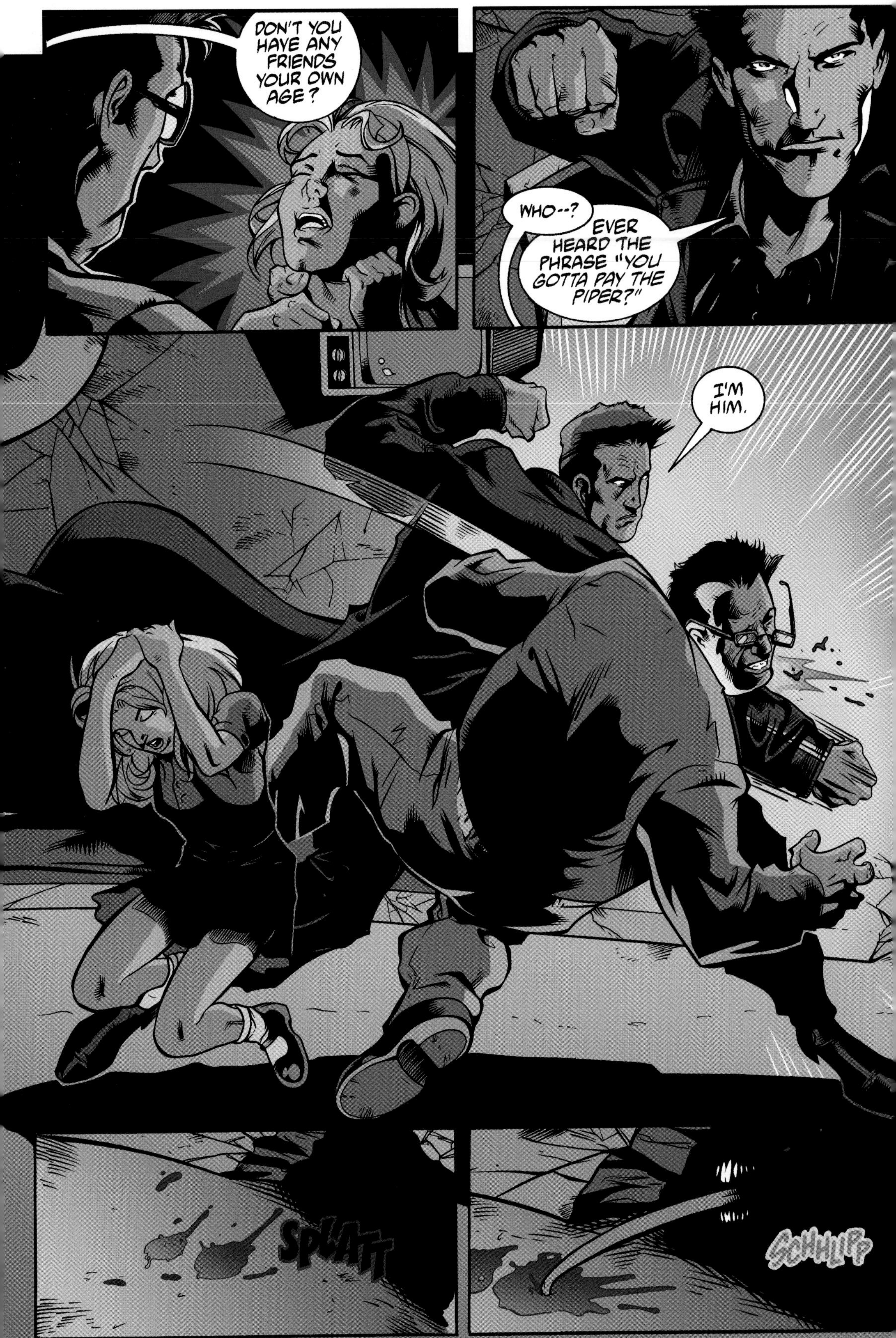
DON'T YOU HAVE ANY FRIENDS YOUR OWN AGE?
WHO--?
EVER HEARD THE PHRASE "YOU GOTTA PAY THE PIPER?"
I'M HIM.
SPLATT
SCHHLIPP

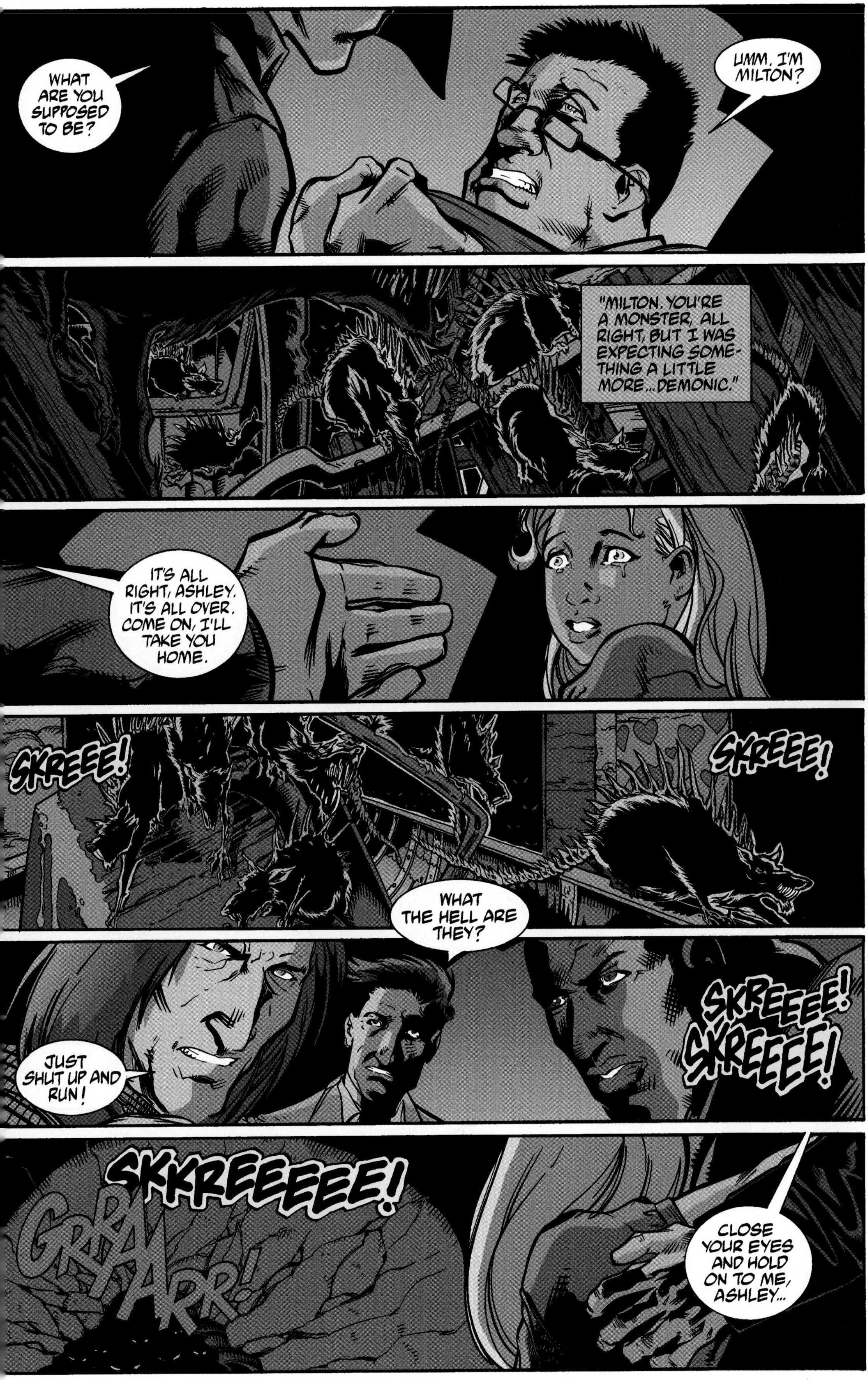
WHAT ARE YOU SUPPOSED TO BE?
UMM. I'M MILTON?
"MILTON. YOU'RE A MONSTER, ALL RIGHT, BUT I WAS EXPECTING SOME-THING A LITTLE MORE...DEMONIC."
IT'S ALL RIGHT, ASHLEY. IT'S ALL OVER. COME ON, I'LL TAKE YOU HOME.
SKREEE!
SKREEE!
WHAT THE HELL ARE THEY?
JUST SHUT UP AND RUN!
SKREEEE! SKREEEE!
SKKREEEEEE!
GRRAARR!
CLOSE YOUR EYES AND HOLD ON TO ME, ASHLEY...

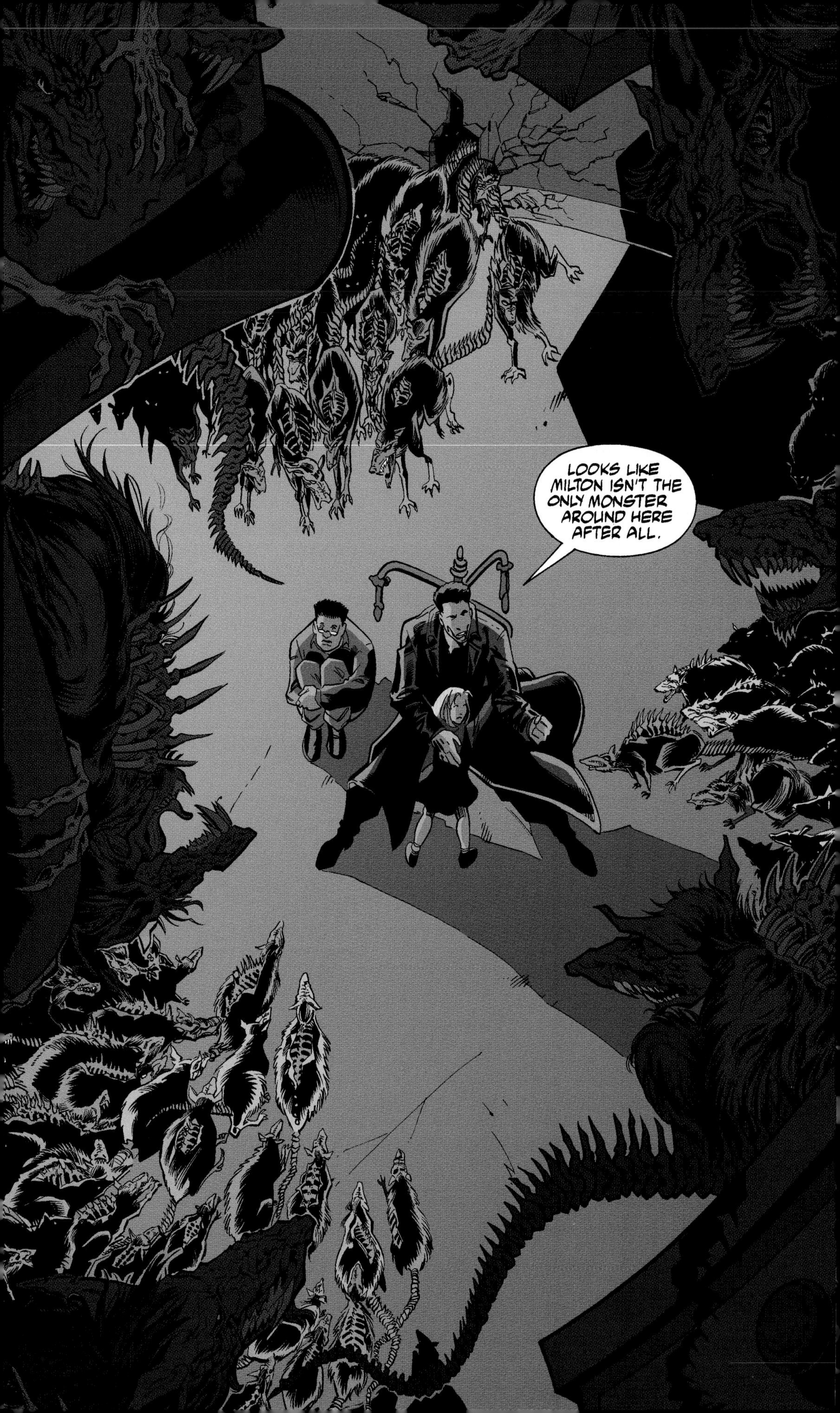
LOOKS LIKE MILTON ISN'T THE ONLY MONSTER AROUND HERE AFTER ALL.

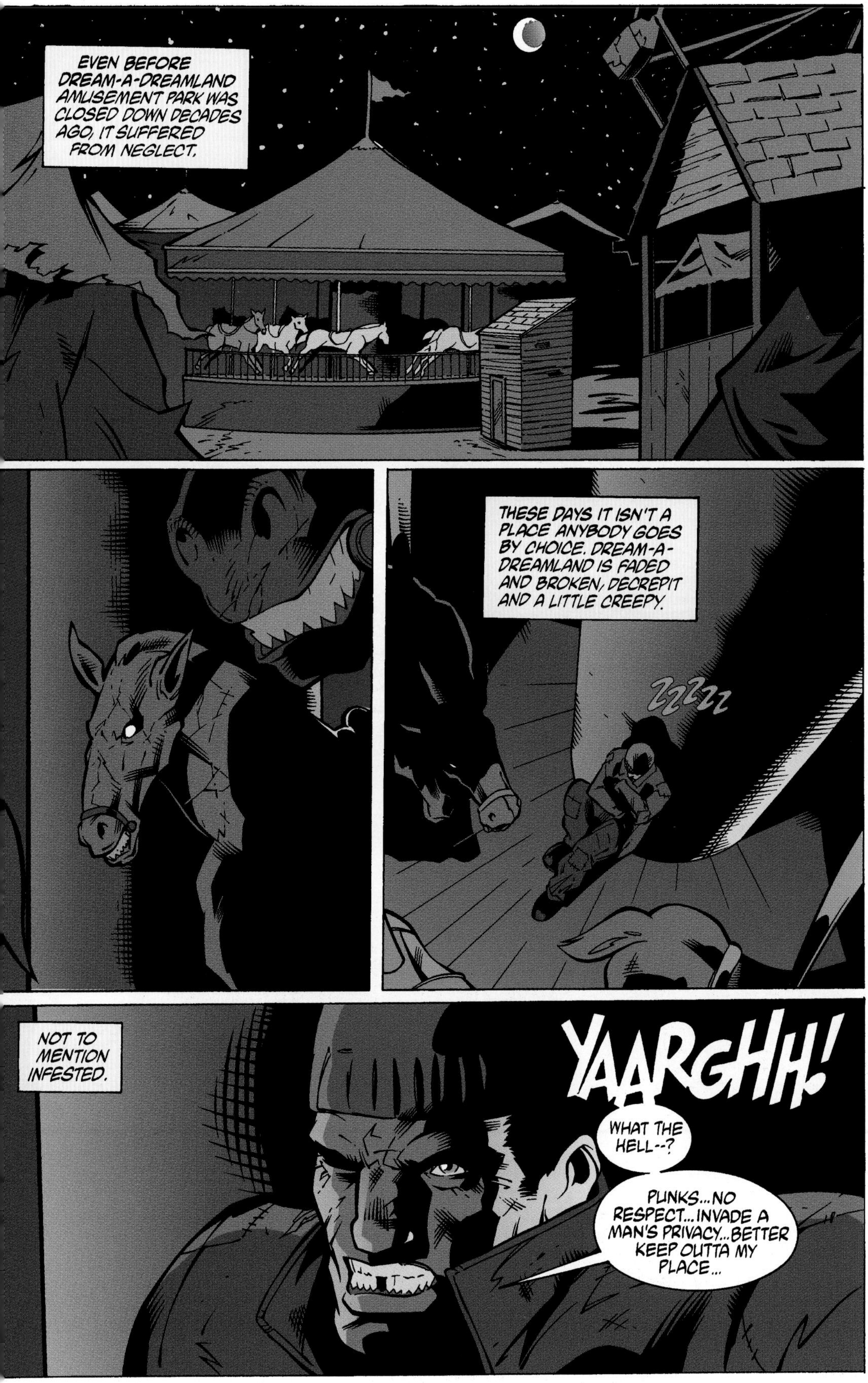
EVEN BEFORE DREAM-A-DREAMLAND AMUSEMENT PARK WAS CLOSED DOWN DECADES AGO, IT SUFFERED FROM NEGLECT.
THESE DAYS IT ISN'T A PLACE ANYBODY GOES BY CHOICE. DREAM-A-DREAMLAND IS FADED AND BROKEN, DECREPIT AND A LITTLE CREEPY.
ZZZZZ
NOT TO MENTION INFESTED.
YAARGHH!
WHAT THE HELL--?
PUNKS...NO RESPECT...INVADE A MAN'S PRIVACY...BETTER KEEP OUTTA MY PLACE...

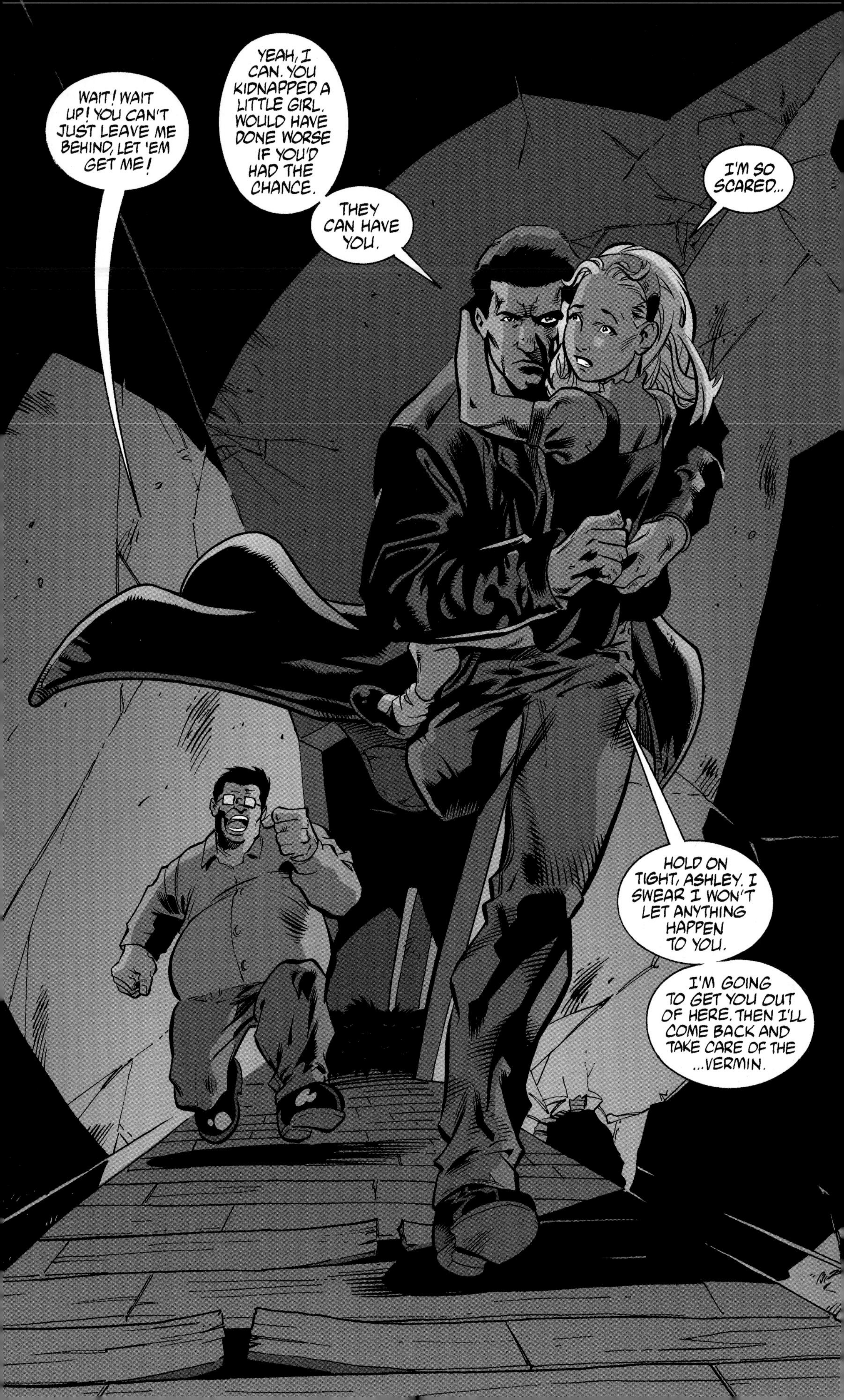
WAIT! WAIT UP! YOU CAN'T JUST LEAVE ME BEHIND, LET 'EM GET ME!
YEAH, I CAN. YOU KIDNAPPED A LITTLE GIRL. WOULD HAVE DONE WORSE IF YOU'D HAD THE CHANCE.
THEY CAN HAVE YOU.
I'M SO SCARED...
HOLD ON TIGHT, ASHLEY. I SWEAR I WON'T LET ANYTHING HAPPEN TO YOU.
I'M GOING TO GET YOU OUT OF HERE. THEN I'LL COME BACK AND TAKE CARE OF THE ...VERMIN.

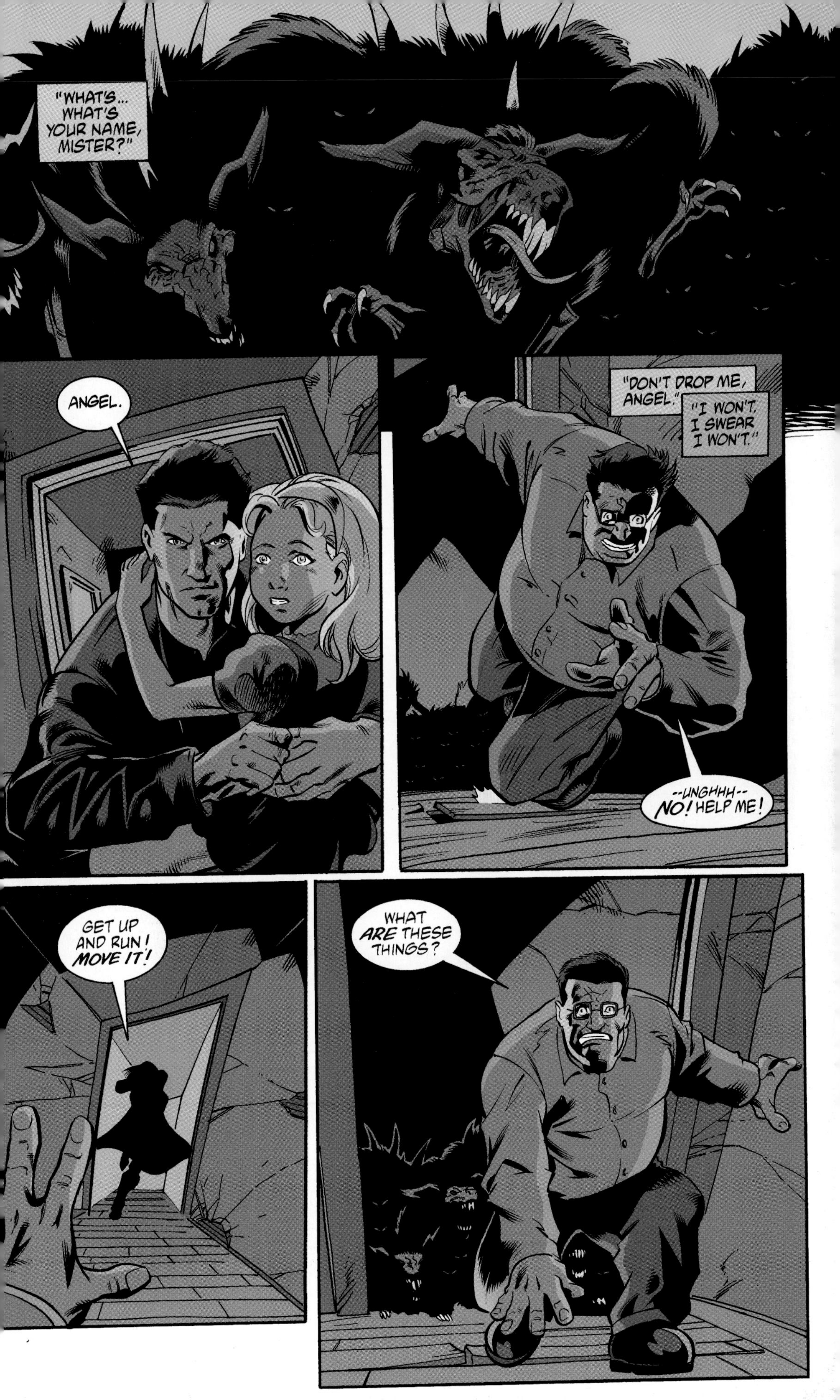
"WHAT'S... WHAT'S YOUR NAME, MISTER?"
ANGEL.
"DON'T DROP ME, ANGEL."
"I WON'T. I SWEAR I WON'T."
--UNGHHH-- NO! HELP ME!
GET UP AND RUN! MOVE IT!
WHAT ARE THESE THINGS?

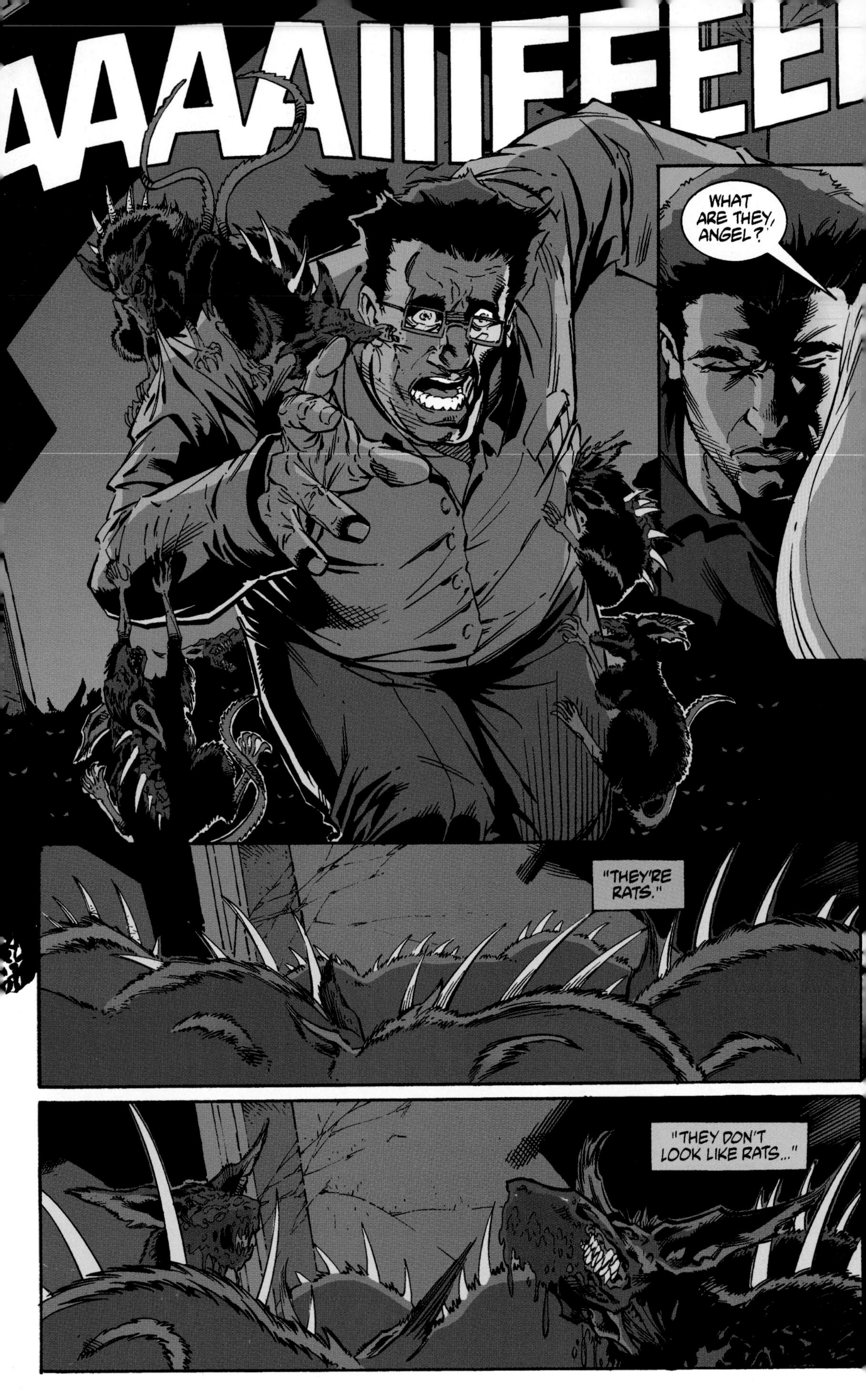
AAAAIIIEEEE
WHAT ARE THEY, ANGEL?
"THEY'RE RATS."
"THEY DON'T LOOK LIKE RATS..."

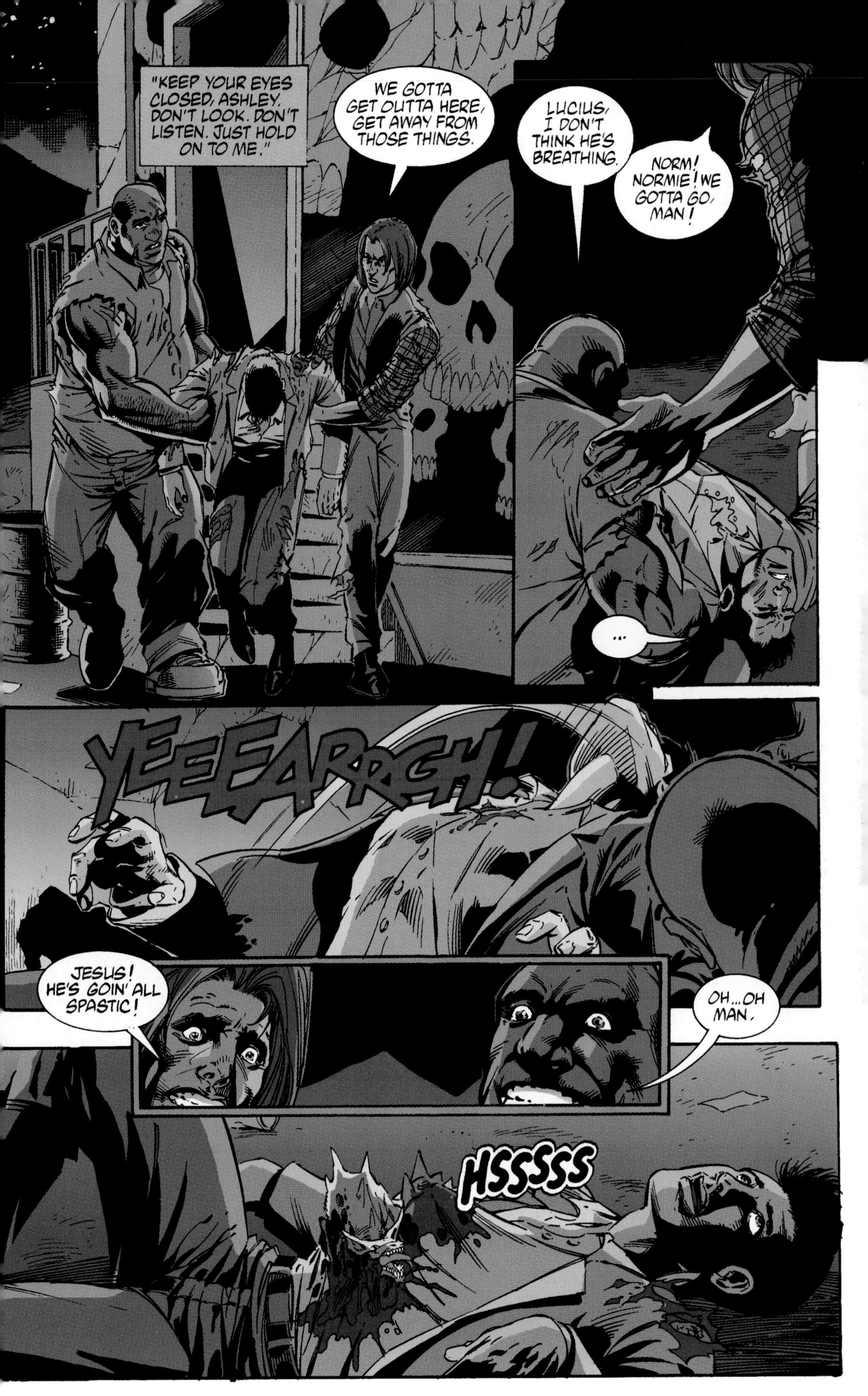
"KEEP YOUR EYES CLOSED, ASHLEY. DON'T LOOK. DON'T LISTEN. JUST HOLD ON TO ME."
WE GOTTA GET OUTTA HERE, GET AWAY FROM THOSE THINGS.
LUCIUS, I DON'T THINK HE'S BREATHING.
NORM! NORMIE! WE GOTTA GO, MAN!
...
YEEEARRGH!
JESUS! HE'S GOIN' ALL SPASTIC!
OH...OH MAN.
HSSSSS

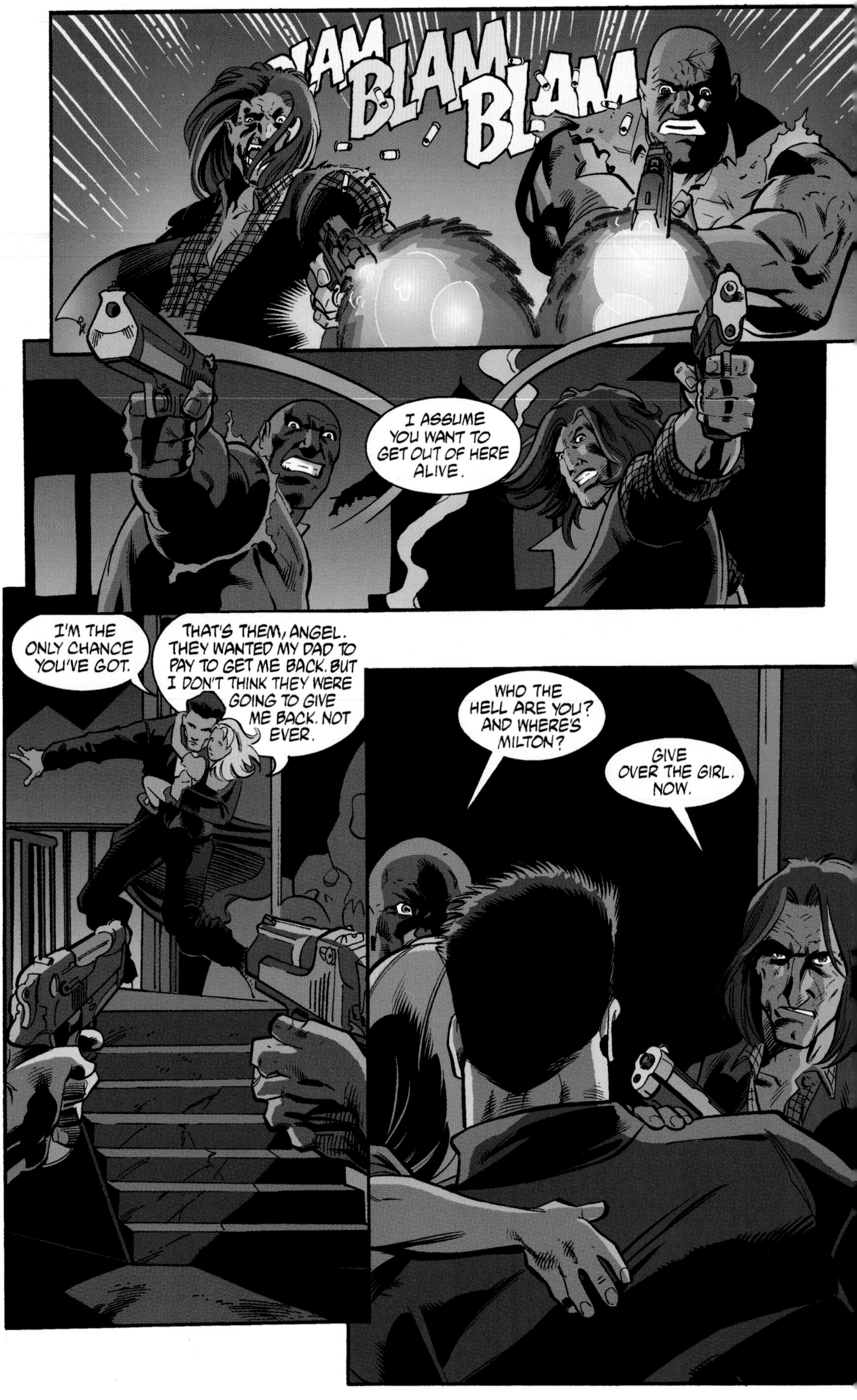
BLAM BLAM BLAM
I ASSUME YOU WANT TO GET OUT OF HERE ALIVE.
I'M THE ONLY CHANCE YOU'VE GOT.
THAT'S THEM, ANGEL. THEY WANTED MY DAD TO PAY TO GET ME BACK. BUT I DON'T THINK THEY WERE GOING TO GIVE ME BACK. NOT EVER.
WHO THE HELL ARE YOU? AND WHERE'S MILTON?
GIVE OVER THE GIRL. NOW.

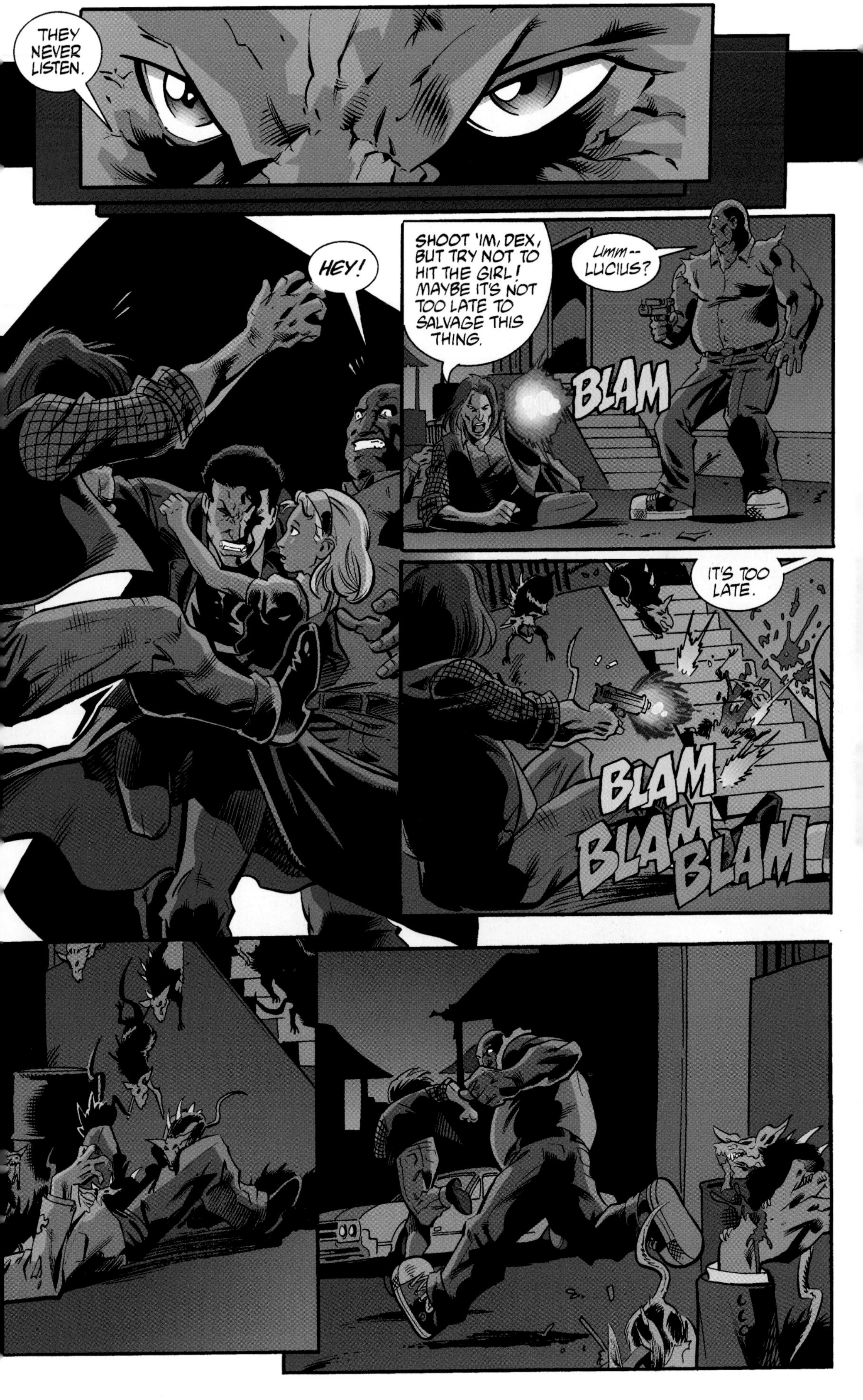
THEY NEVER LISTEN.
HEY!
SHOOT 'IM, DEX, BUT TRY NOT TO HIT THE GIRL! MAYBE IT'S NOT TOO LATE TO SALVAGE THIS THING.
UMM-- LUCIUS?
BLAM
IT'S TOO LATE.
BLAM
BLAM
BLAM!

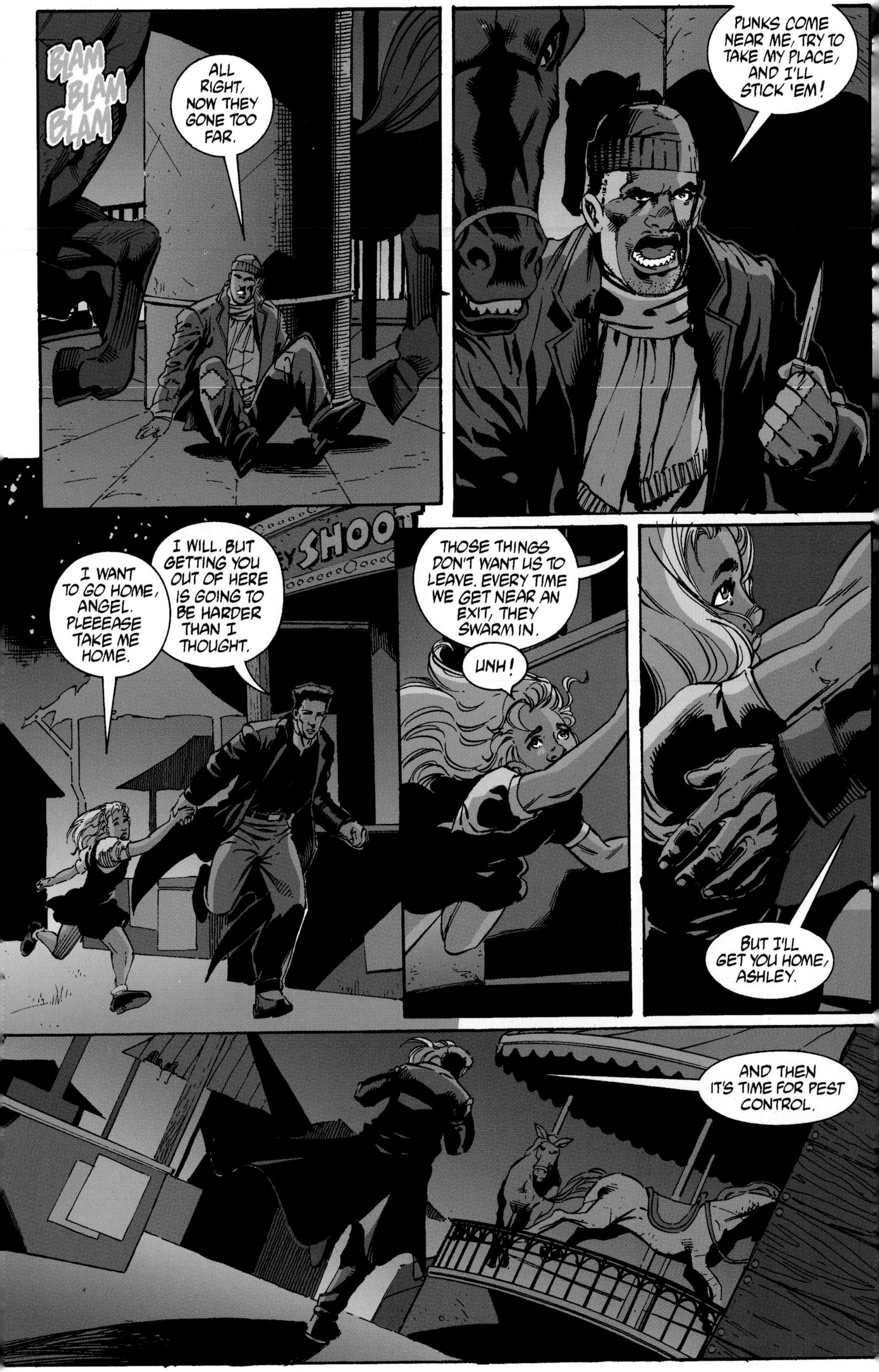
BLAM BLAM BLAM
ALL RIGHT, NOW THEY GONE TOO FAR.
PUNKS COME NEAR ME, TRY TO TAKE MY PLACE, AND I'LL STICK 'EM!
I WANT TO GO HOME, ANGEL. PLEEEASE TAKE ME HOME.
I WILL. BUT GETTING YOU OUT OF HERE IS GOING TO BE HARDER THAN I THOUGHT.
SHOOT
THOSE THINGS DON'T WANT US TO LEAVE. EVERY TIME WE GET NEAR AN EXIT, THEY SWARM IN.
UNH!
BUT I'LL GET YOU HOME, ASHLEY.
AND THEN IT'S TIME FOR PEST CONTROL.

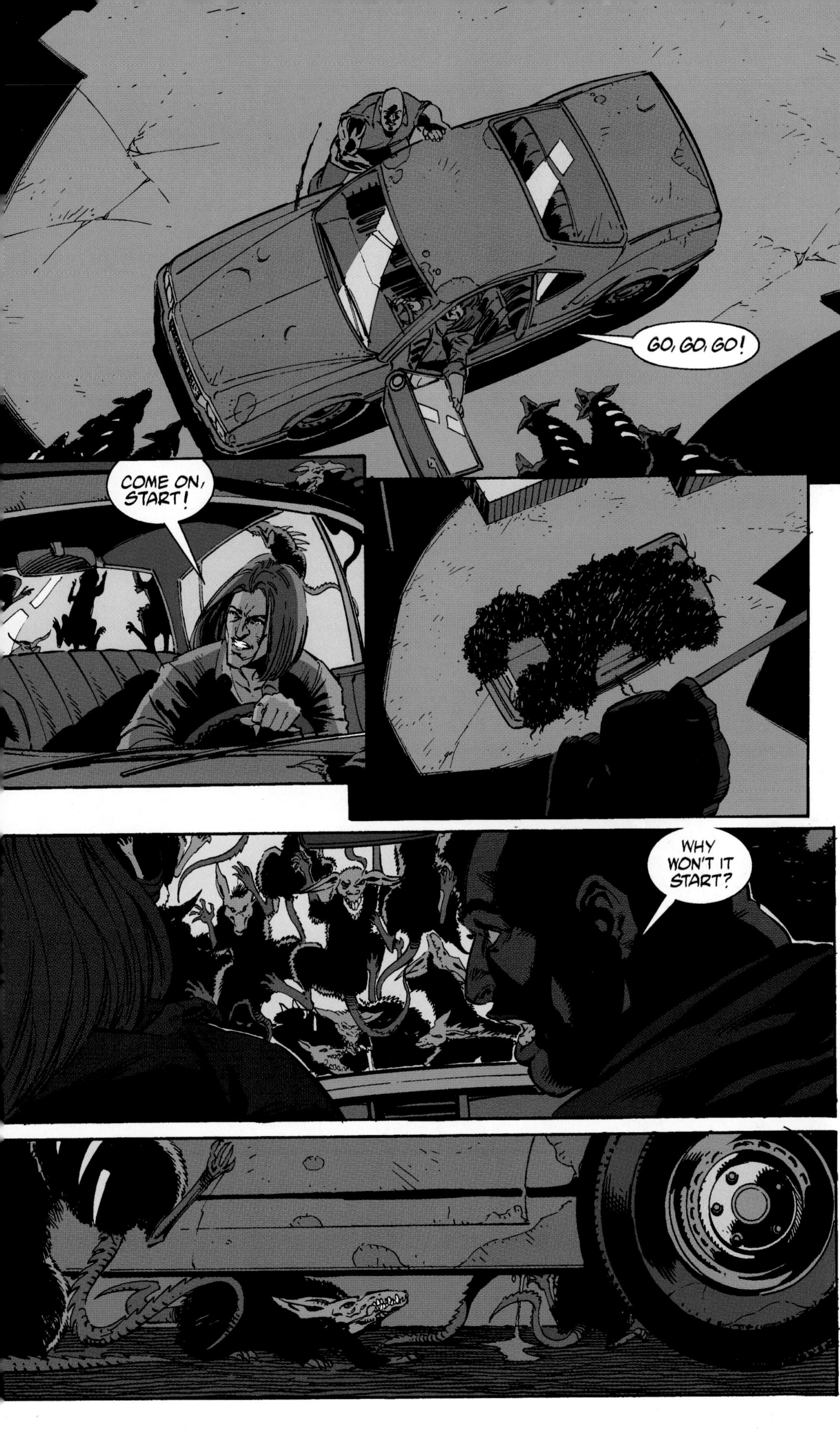
GO, GO, GO!
COME ON, START!
WHY WON'T IT START?

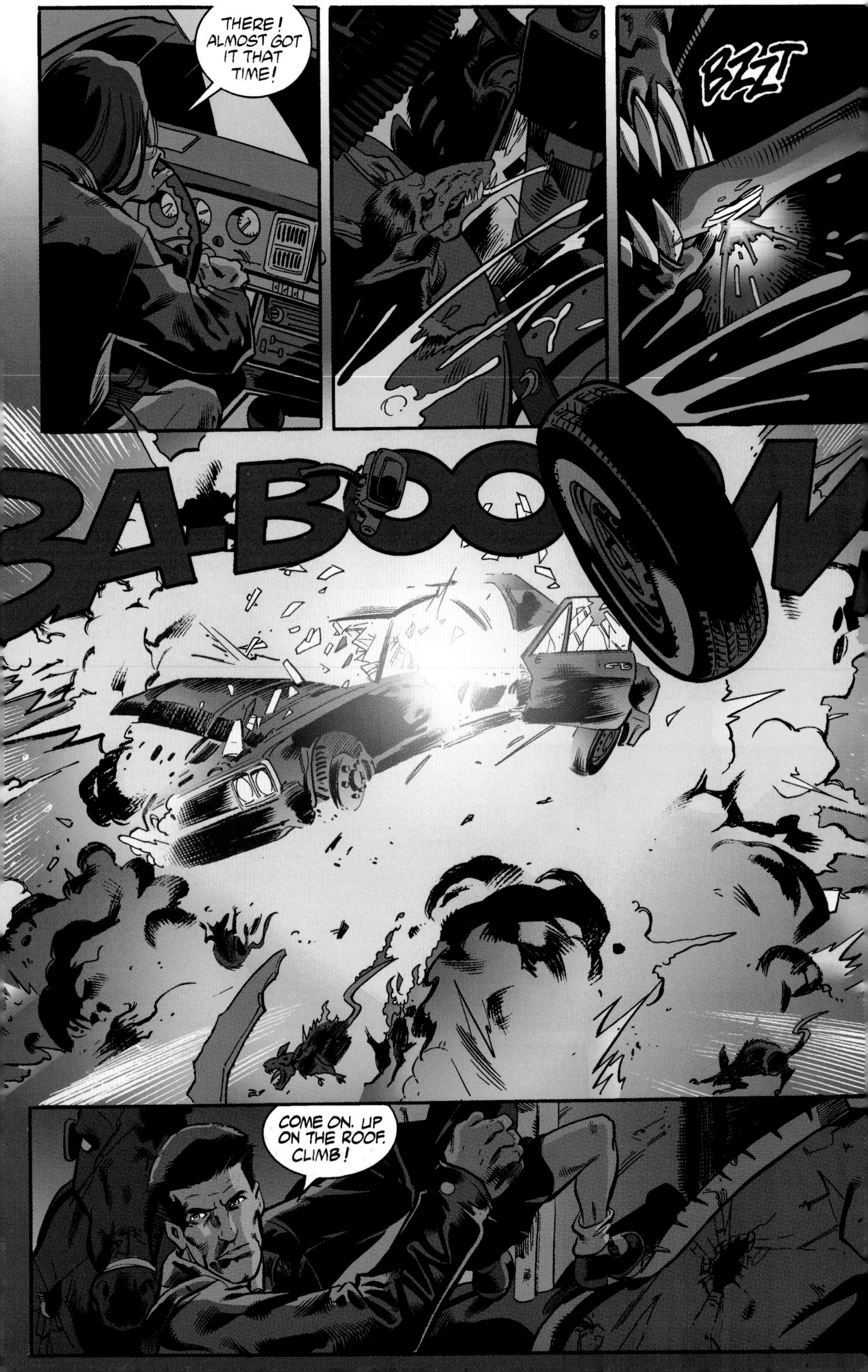
THERE! ALMOST GOT IT THAT TIME!
BZZT
BA-BOOM
COME ON. UP ON THE ROOF. CLIMB!

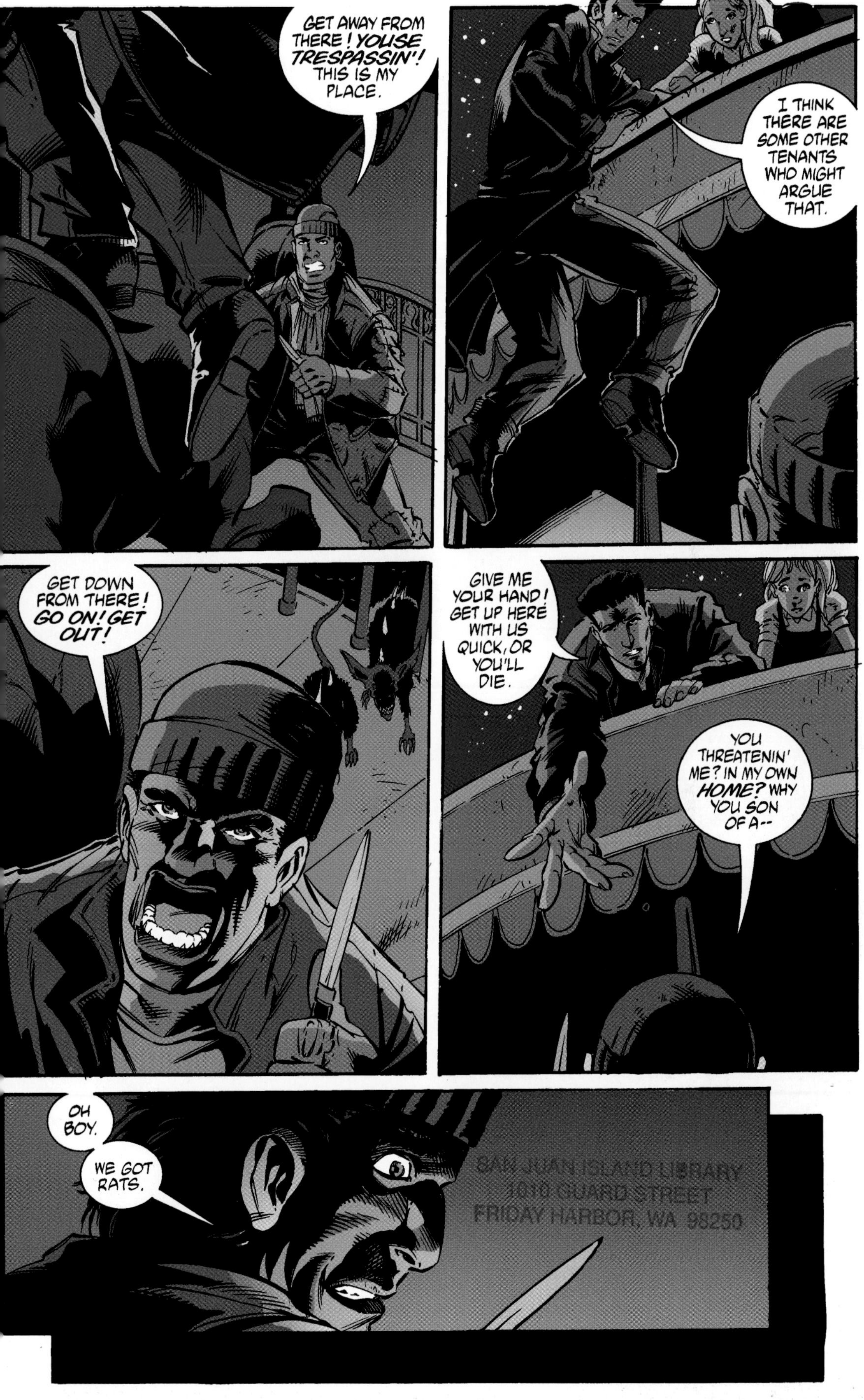
GET AWAY FROM THERE! *YOUSE TRESPASSIN'!* THIS IS MY PLACE.
I THINK THERE ARE SOME OTHER TENANTS WHO MIGHT ARGUE THAT.
GET DOWN FROM THERE! *GO ON! GET OUT!*
GIVE ME YOUR HAND! GET UP HERE WITH US QUICK, OR YOU'LL DIE.
YOU THREATENIN' ME? IN MY OWN *HOME?* WHY YOU SON OF A--
OH BOY.
WE GOT RATS.

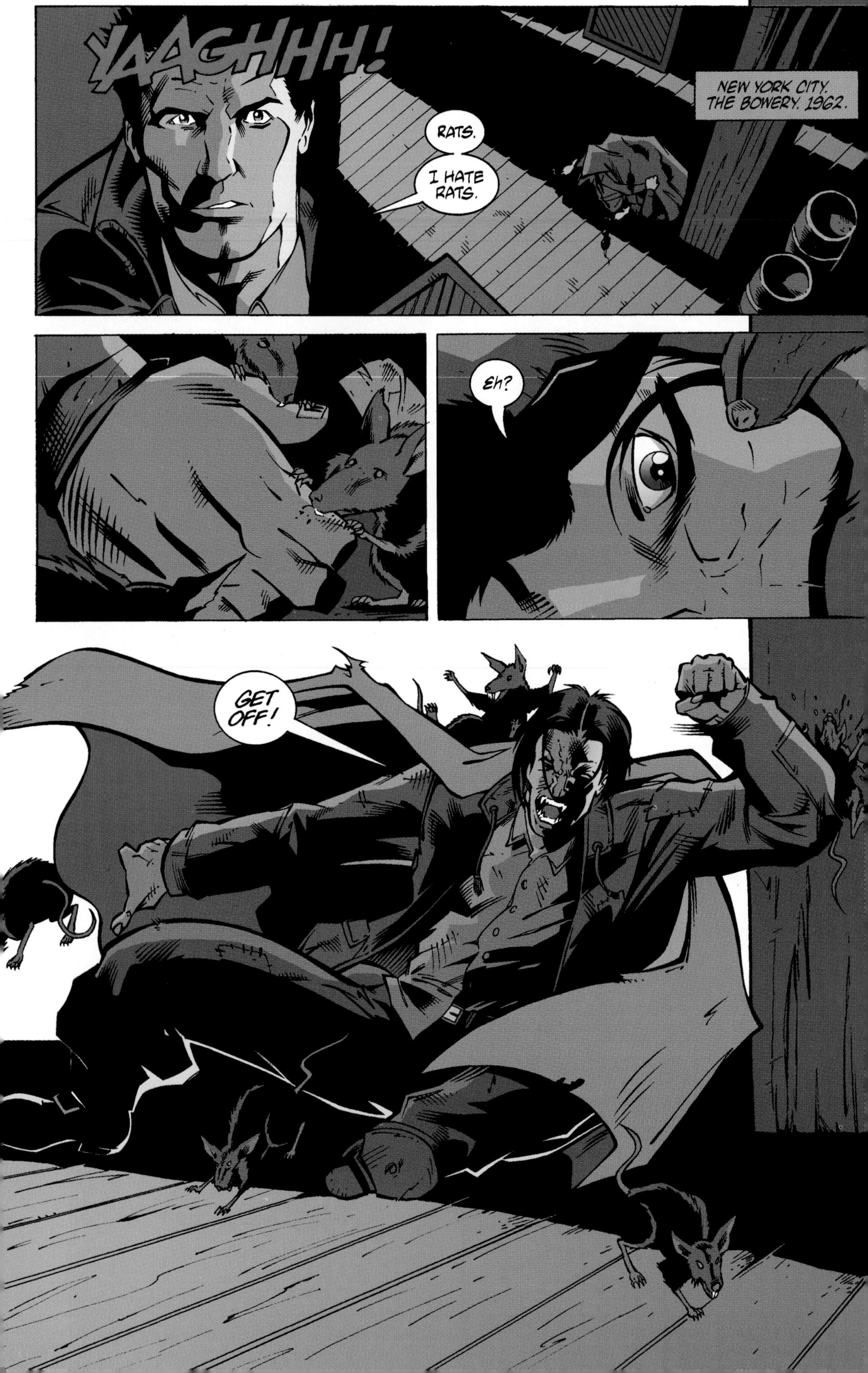
YAAGHHH!
NEW YORK CITY. THE BOWERY. 1962.
RATS.
I HATE RATS.
Eh?
GET OFF!

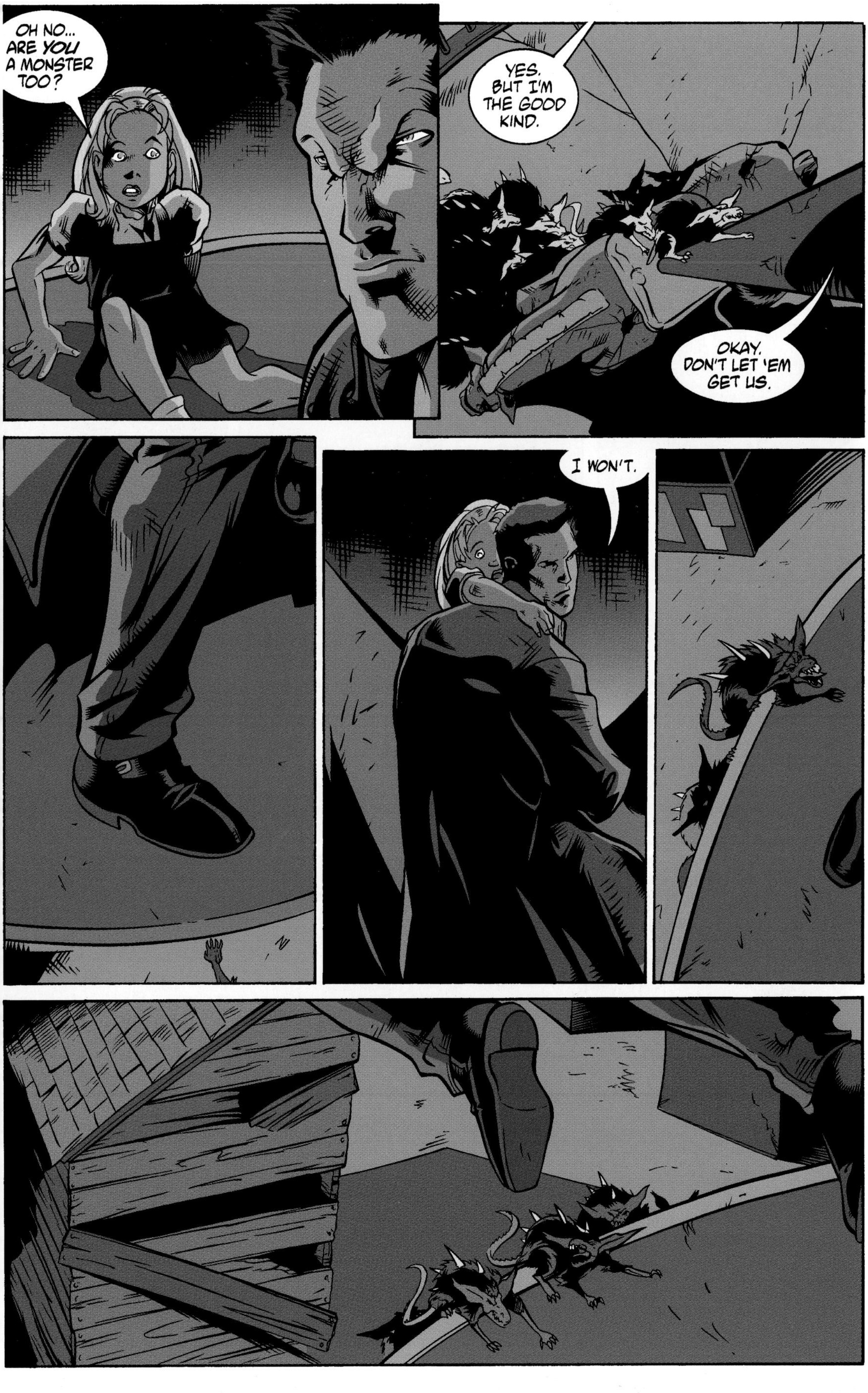
OH NO... ARE YOU A MONSTER TOO?
YES. BUT I'M THE GOOD KIND.
OKAY. DON'T LET 'EM GET US.
I WON'T.

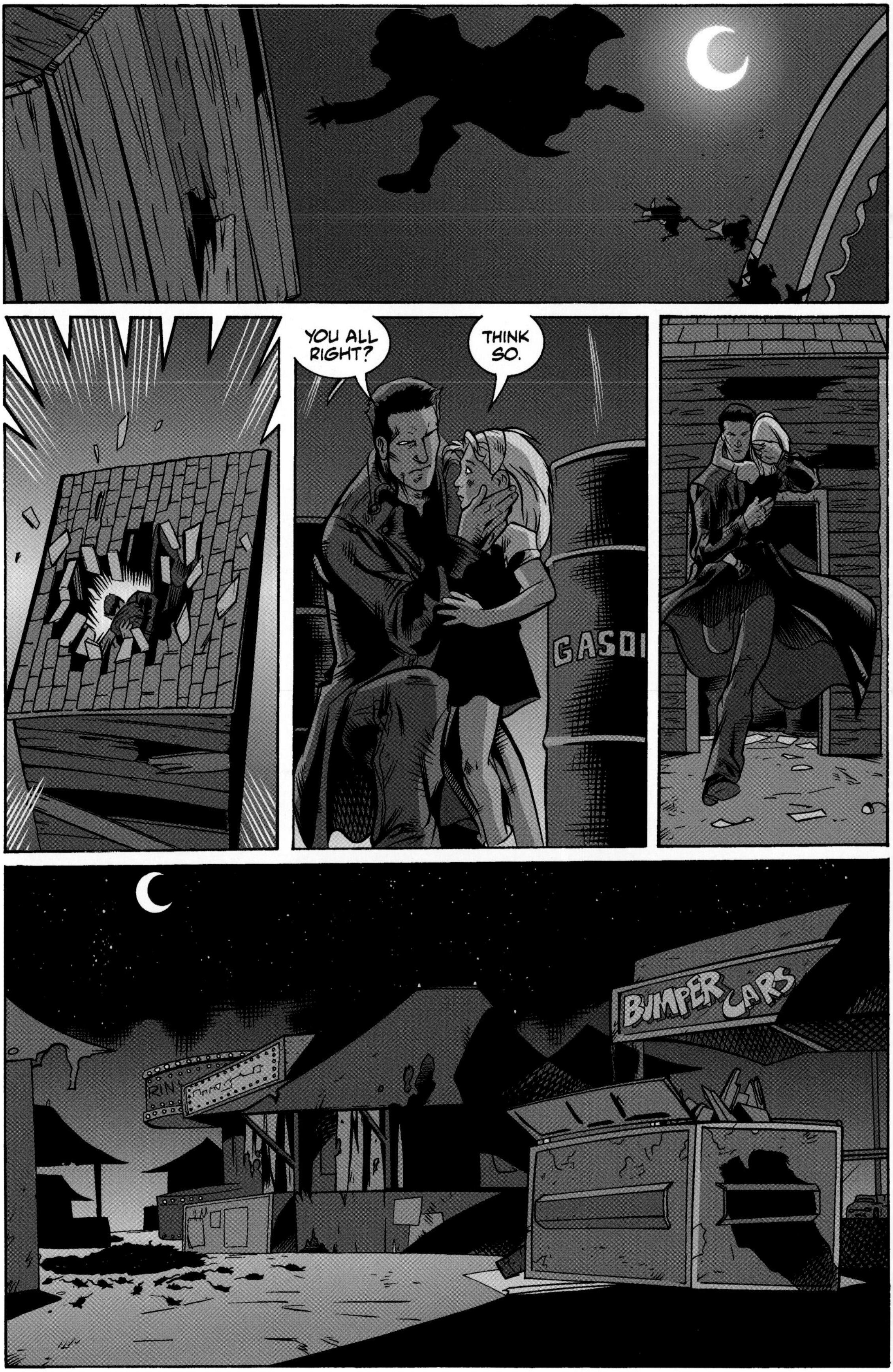
YOU ALL RIGHT?
THINK SO.
GASO
BUMPER CARS
RIN

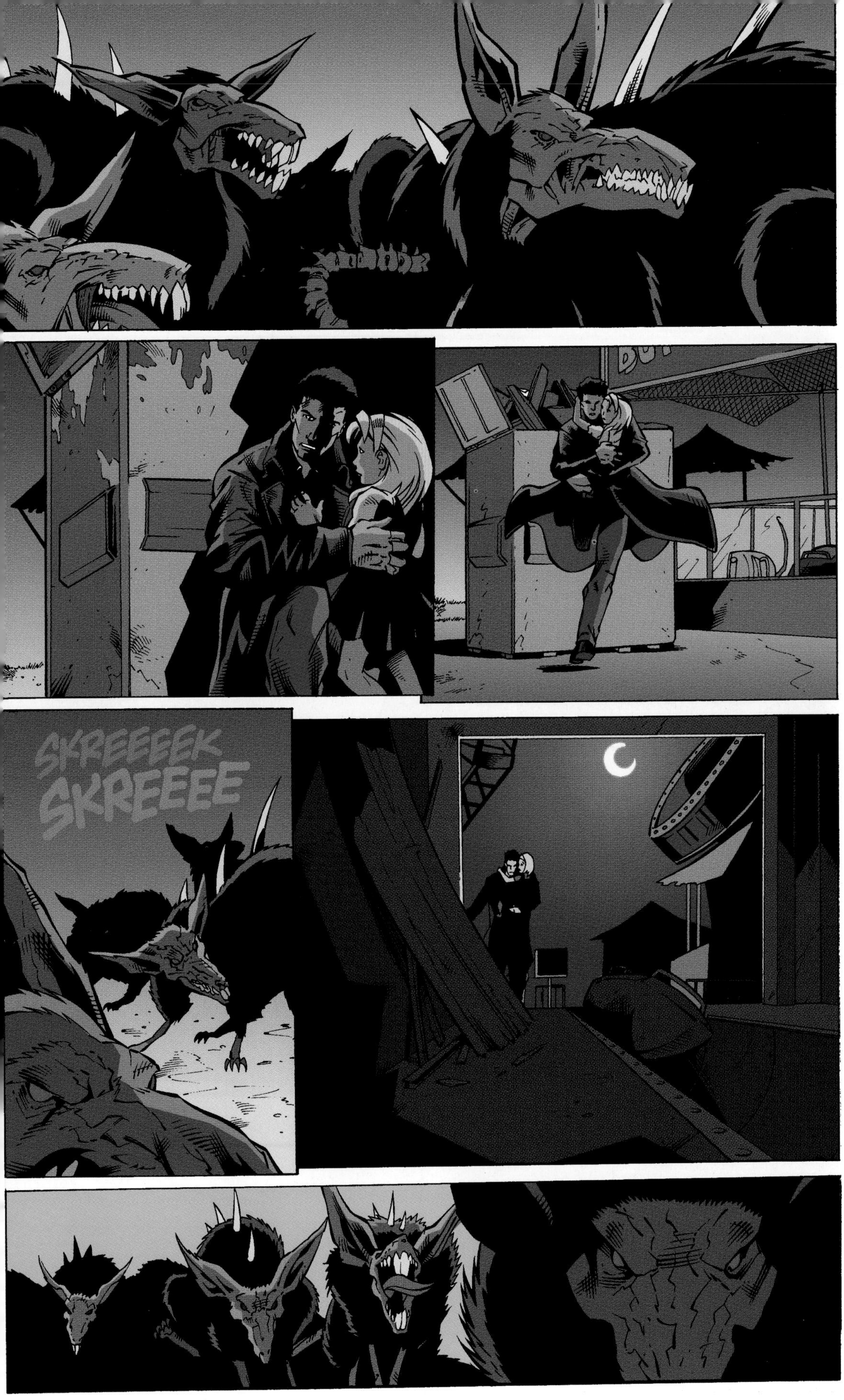
SKREEEEK
SKREEEE

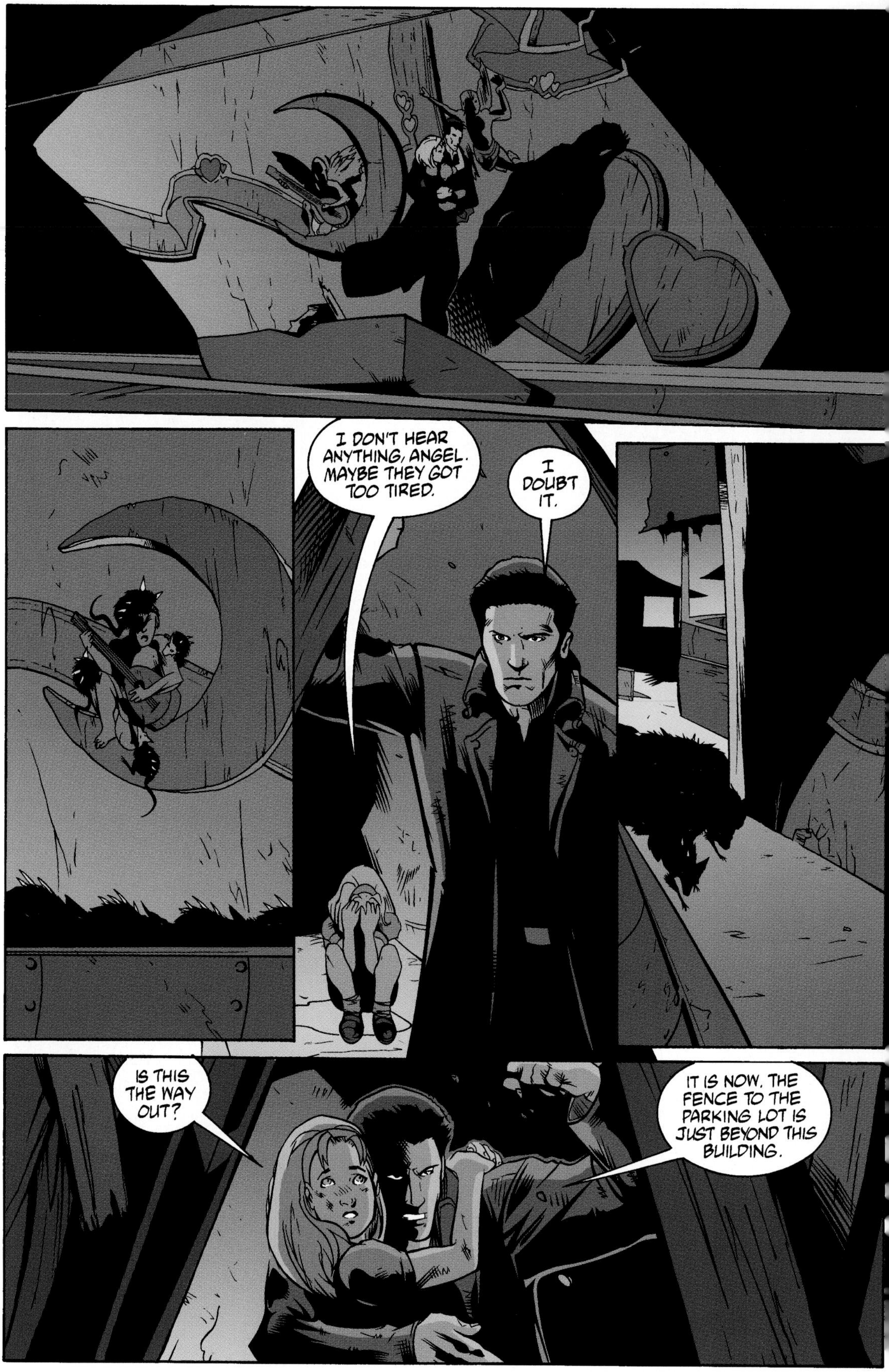

I DON'T HEAR ANYTHING, ANGEL. MAYBE THEY GOT TOO TIRED.
I DOUBT IT.
IS THIS THE WAY OUT?
IT IS NOW. THE FENCE TO THE PARKING LOT IS JUST BEYOND THIS BUILDING.

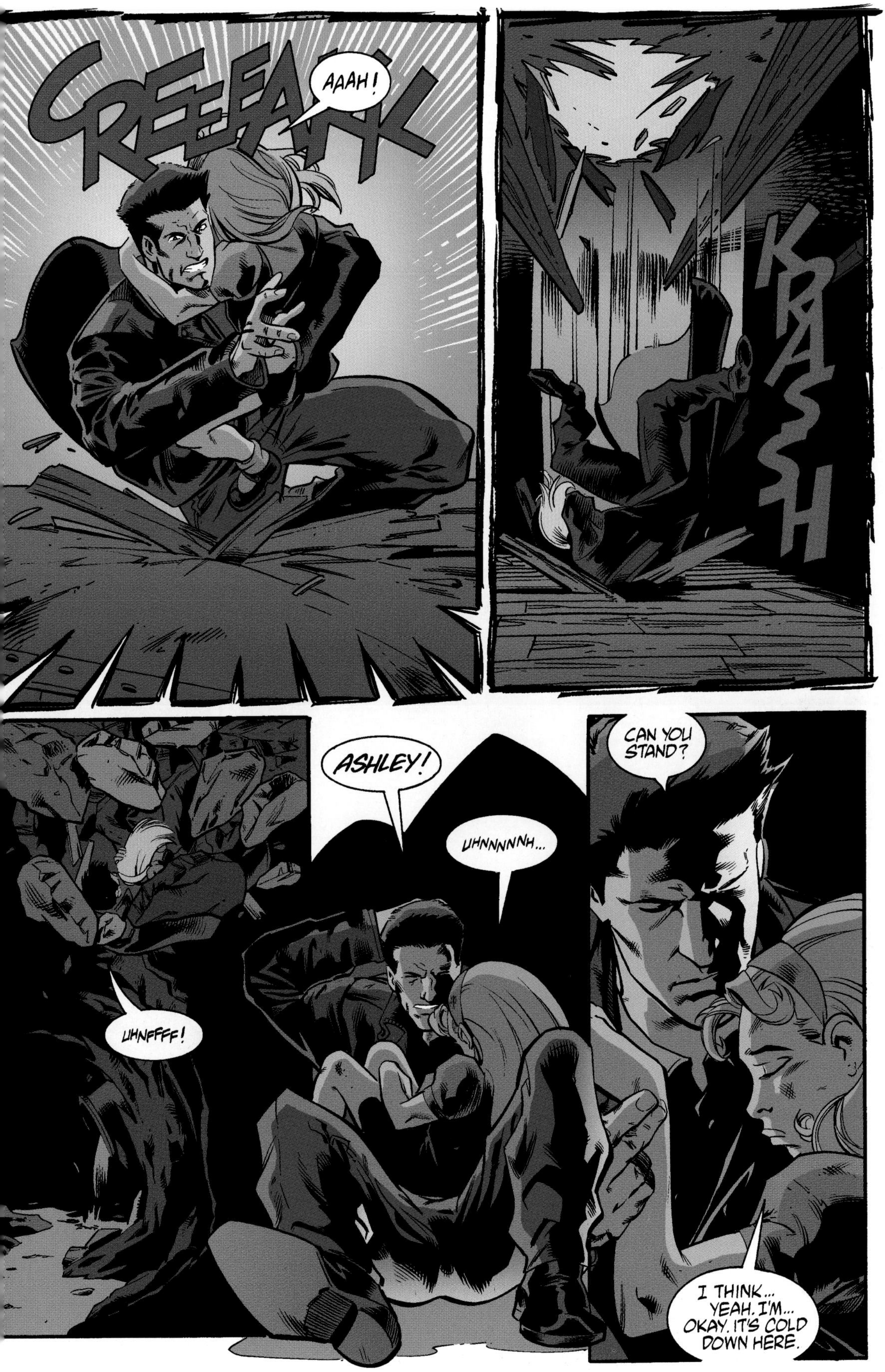
CREEEAAAK
AAAH!
KRASH
ASHLEY!
UHNNNNNH...
UHNFFFF!
CAN YOU STAND?
I THINK... YEAH. I'M... OKAY. IT'S COLD DOWN HERE.

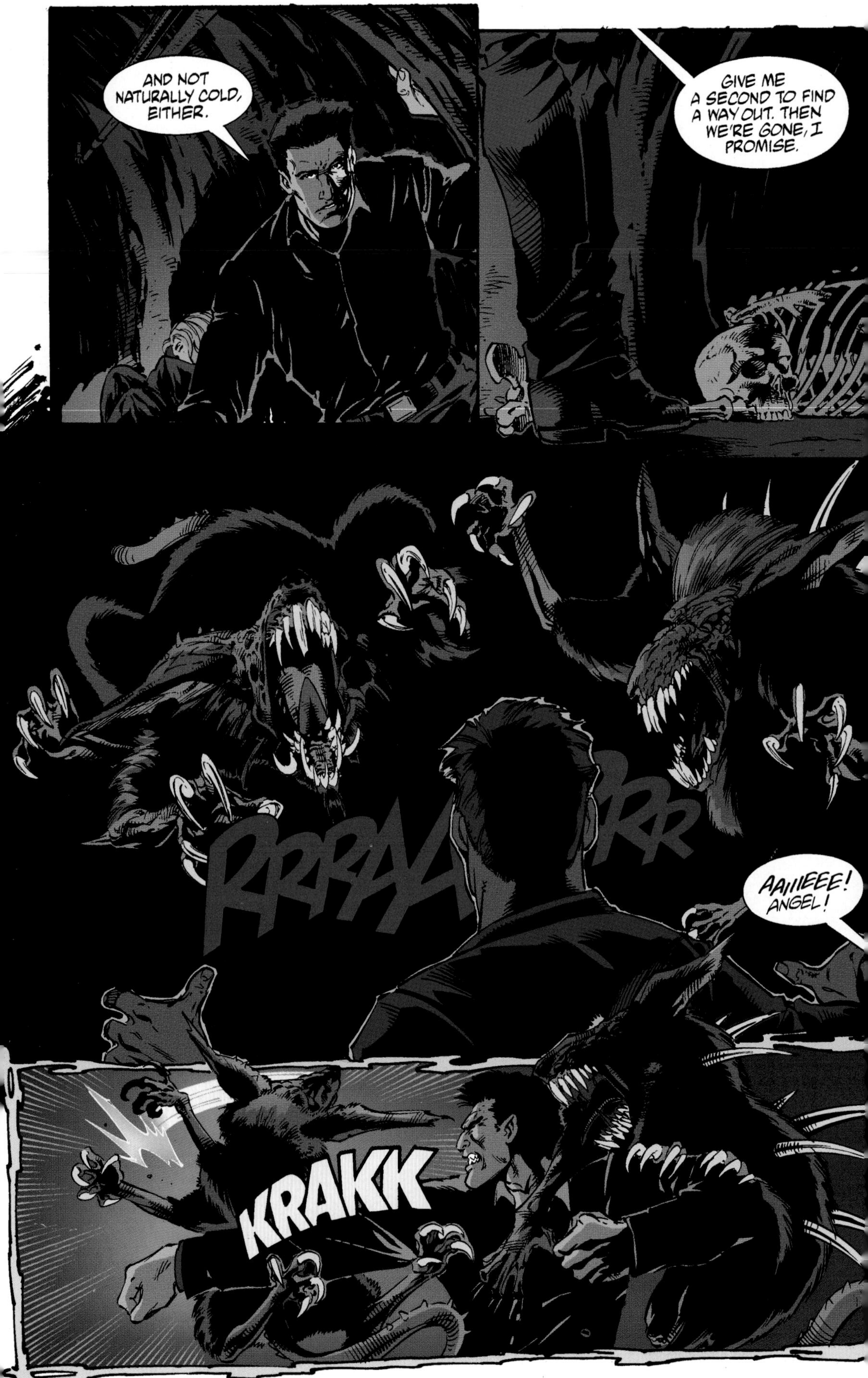
AND NOT NATURALLY COLD, EITHER.
GIVE ME A SECOND TO FIND A WAY OUT. THEN WE'RE GONE, I PROMISE.
RRRAARRR
AAIIIEEE! ANGEL!
KRAKK

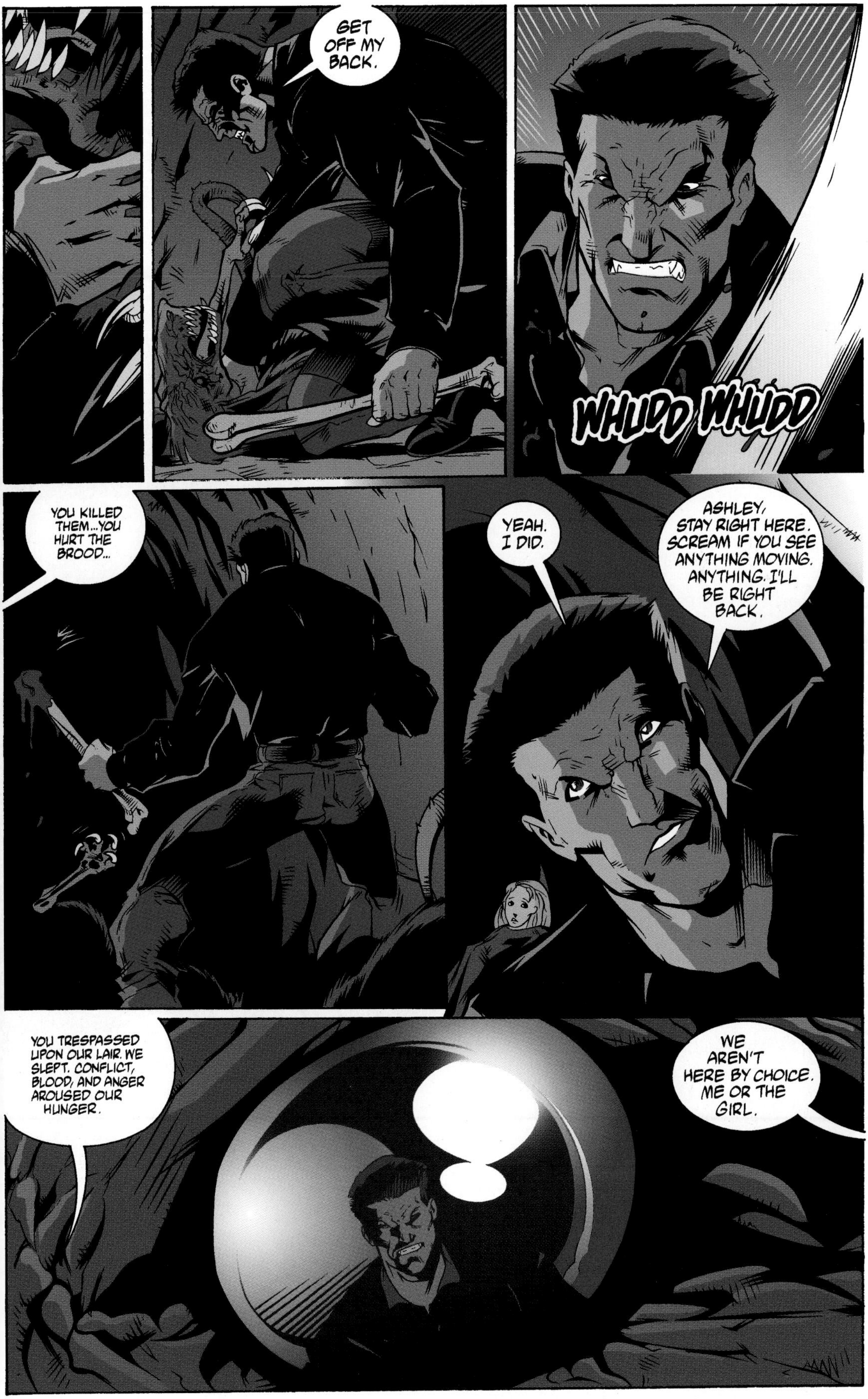
GET OFF MY BACK.
WHUDD WHUDD
YOU KILLED THEM...YOU HURT THE BROOD...
YEAH. I DID.
ASHLEY, STAY RIGHT HERE. SCREAM IF YOU SEE ANYTHING MOVING. ANYTHING. I'LL BE RIGHT BACK.
YOU TRESPASSED UPON OUR LAIR. WE SLEPT. CONFLICT, BLOOD, AND ANGER AROUSED OUR HUNGER.
WE AREN'T HERE BY CHOICE. ME OR THE GIRL.

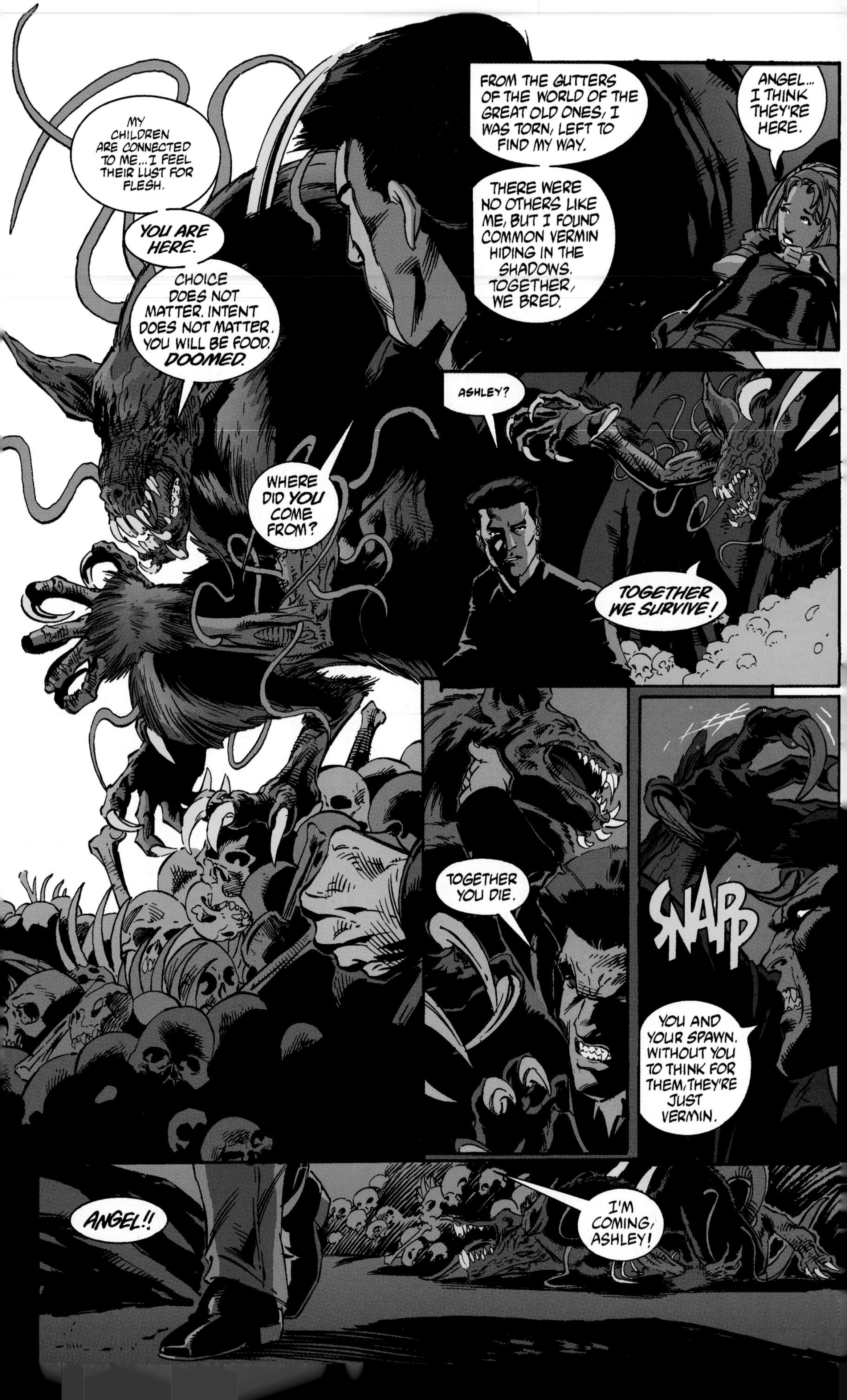

MY CHILDREN ARE CONNECTED TO ME...I FEEL THEIR LUST FOR FLESH.
YOU ARE HERE.
CHOICE DOES NOT MATTER. INTENT DOES NOT MATTER. YOU WILL BE FOOD. DOOMED.
FROM THE GUTTERS OF THE WORLD OF THE GREAT OLD ONES, I WAS TORN, LEFT TO FIND MY WAY.
THERE WERE NO OTHERS LIKE ME, BUT I FOUND COMMON VERMIN HIDING IN THE SHADOWS. TOGETHER, WE BRED.
ANGEL... I THINK THEY'RE HERE.
WHERE DID YOU COME FROM?
ASHLEY?
TOGETHER WE SURVIVE!
TOGETHER YOU DIE.
SNAP
YOU AND YOUR SPAWN. WITHOUT YOU TO THINK FOR THEM, THEY'RE JUST VERMIN.
ANGEL!!
I'M COMING, ASHLEY!

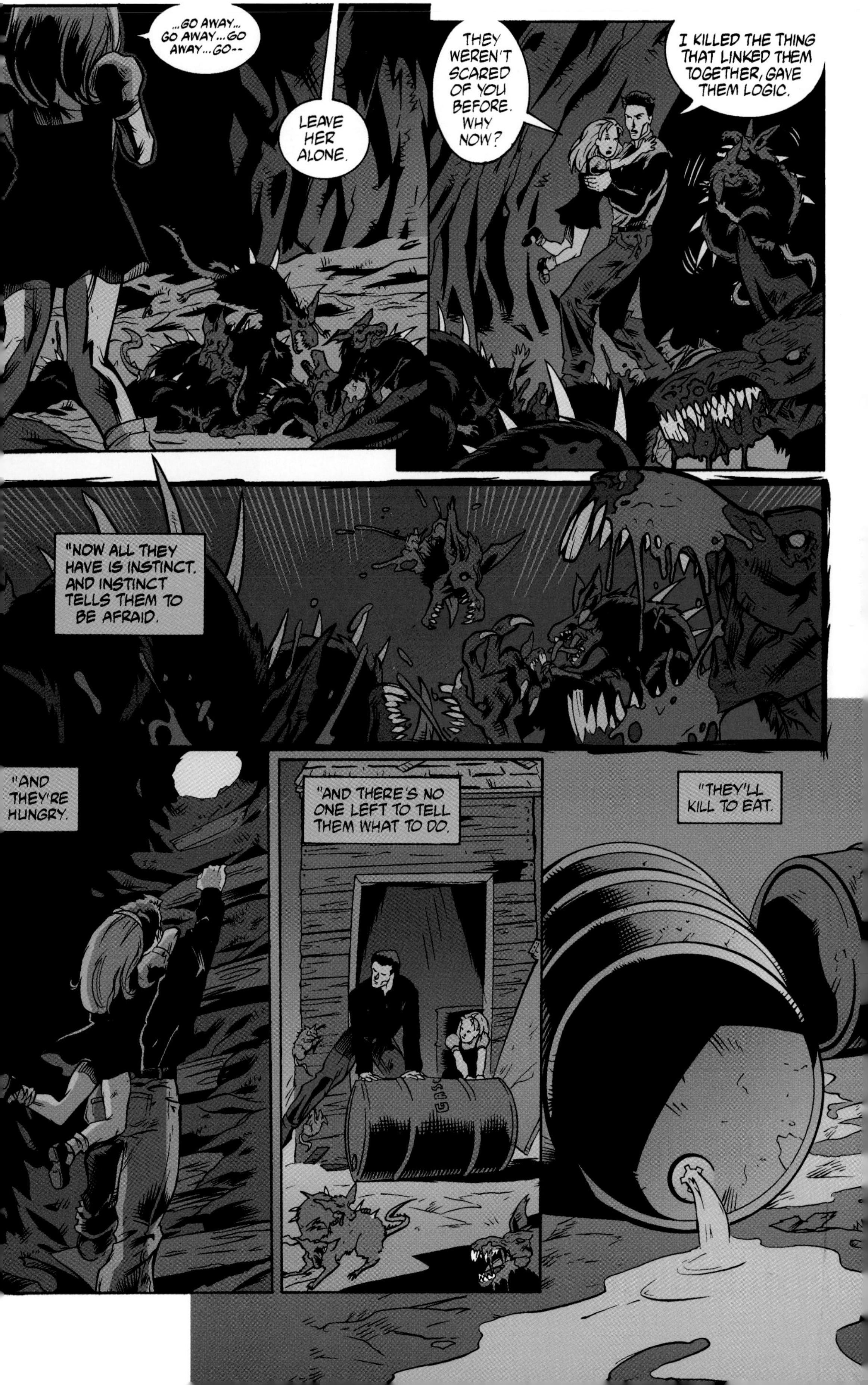
...GO AWAY... GO AWAY... GO AWAY... GO--
LEAVE HER ALONE.
THEY WEREN'T SCARED OF YOU BEFORE. WHY NOW?
I KILLED THE THING THAT LINKED THEM TOGETHER, GAVE THEM LOGIC.
"NOW ALL THEY HAVE IS INSTINCT. AND INSTINCT TELLS THEM TO BE AFRAID.
"AND THEY'RE HUNGRY.
"AND THERE'S NO ONE LEFT TO TELL THEM WHAT TO DO.
"THEY'LL KILL TO EAT.

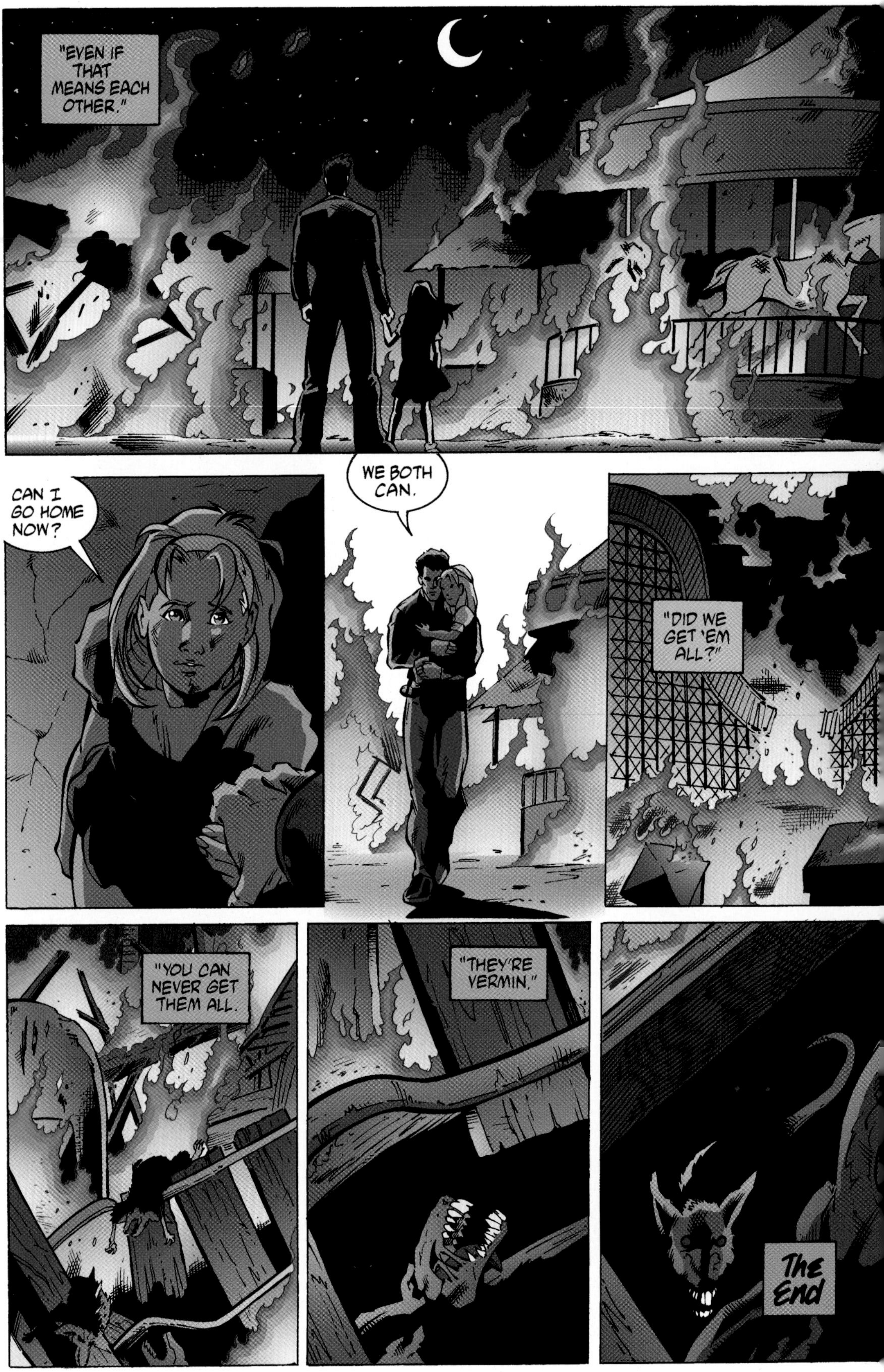
"EVEN IF THAT MEANS EACH OTHER."
CAN I GO HOME NOW?
WE BOTH CAN.
"DID WE GET 'EM ALL?"
"YOU CAN NEVER GET THEM ALL.
"THEY'RE VERMIN."
The End

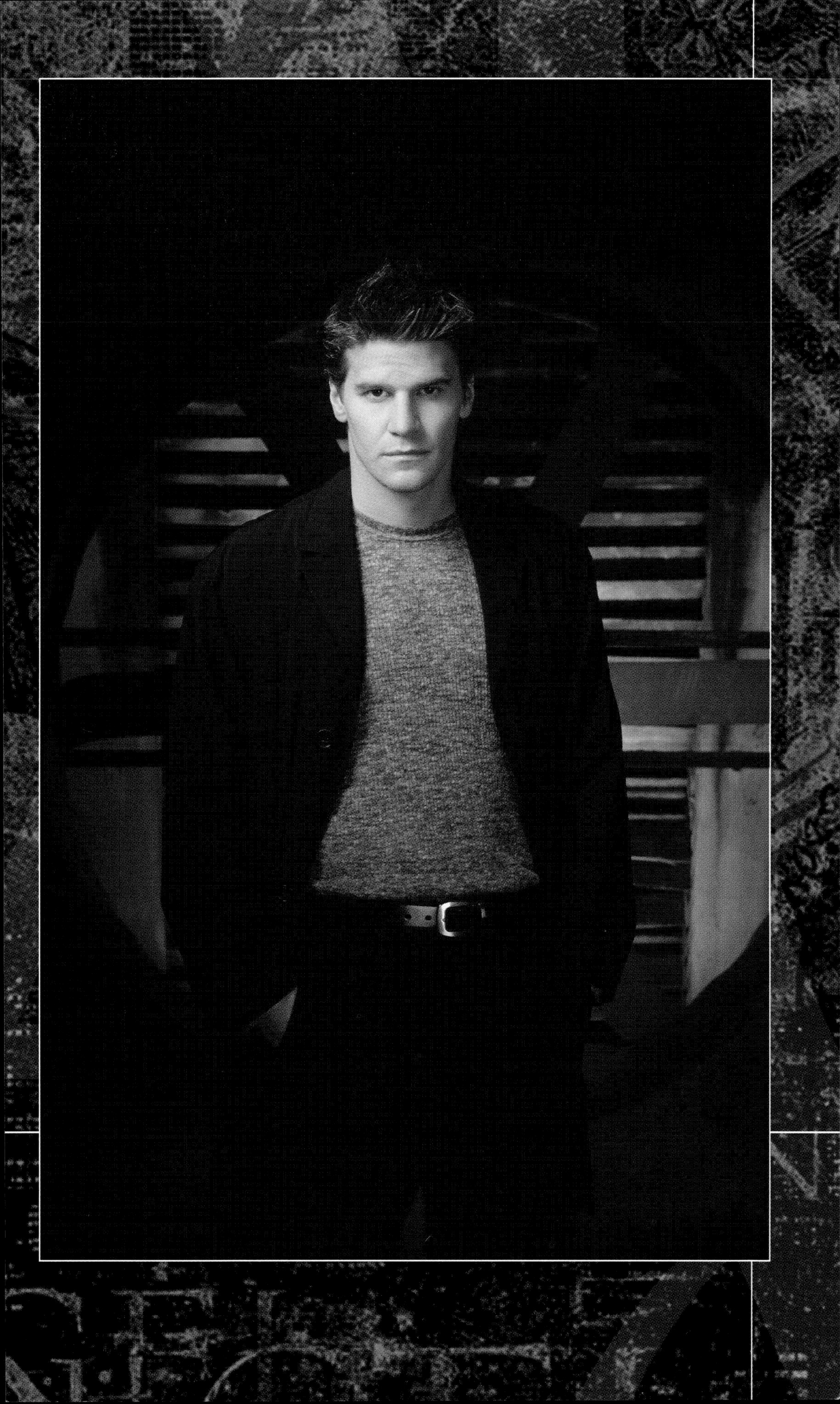

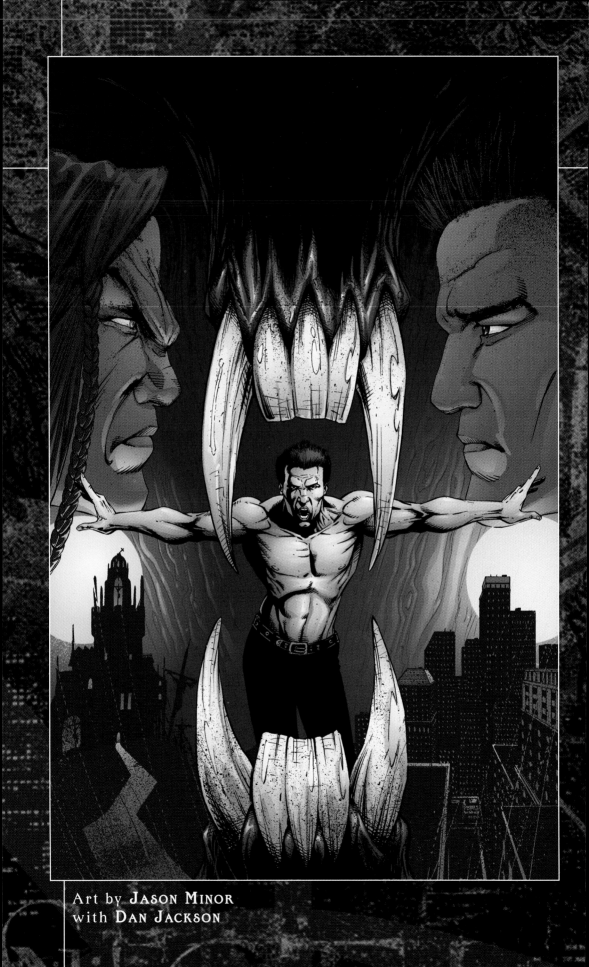

Art by JASON MINOR
with DAN JACKSON

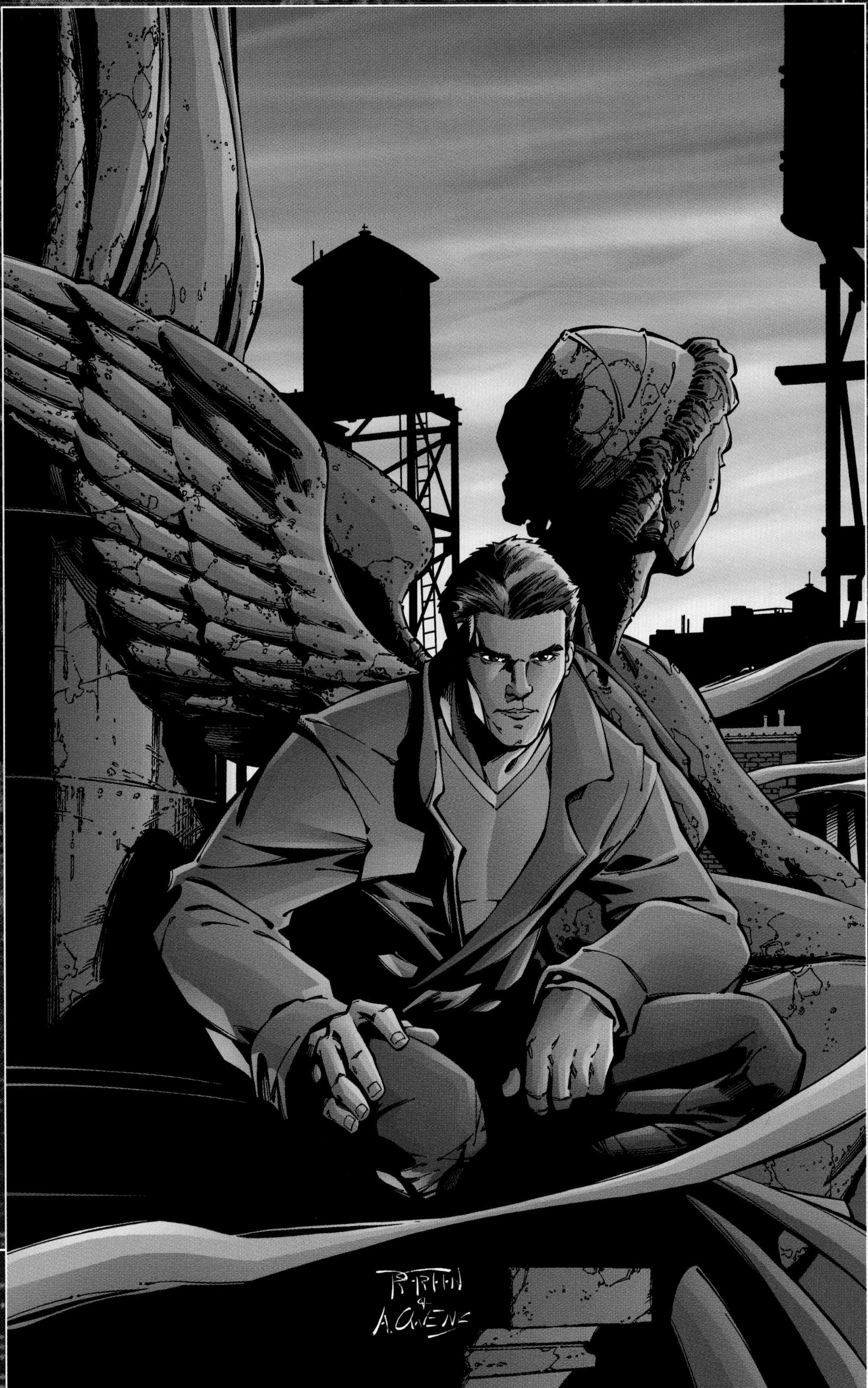
R.GREEN
&
A. OWENS

Art by RANDY GREEN
with ANDY OWENS and DAVE STEWART

Little Girl Lost

writers
CHRISTOPHER GOLDEN
and TOM SNIEGOSKI

penciller
ERIC POWELL

inker
JASON MOORE

colorist
LEE LOUGHRIDGE

letterer
PAT BROSSEAU

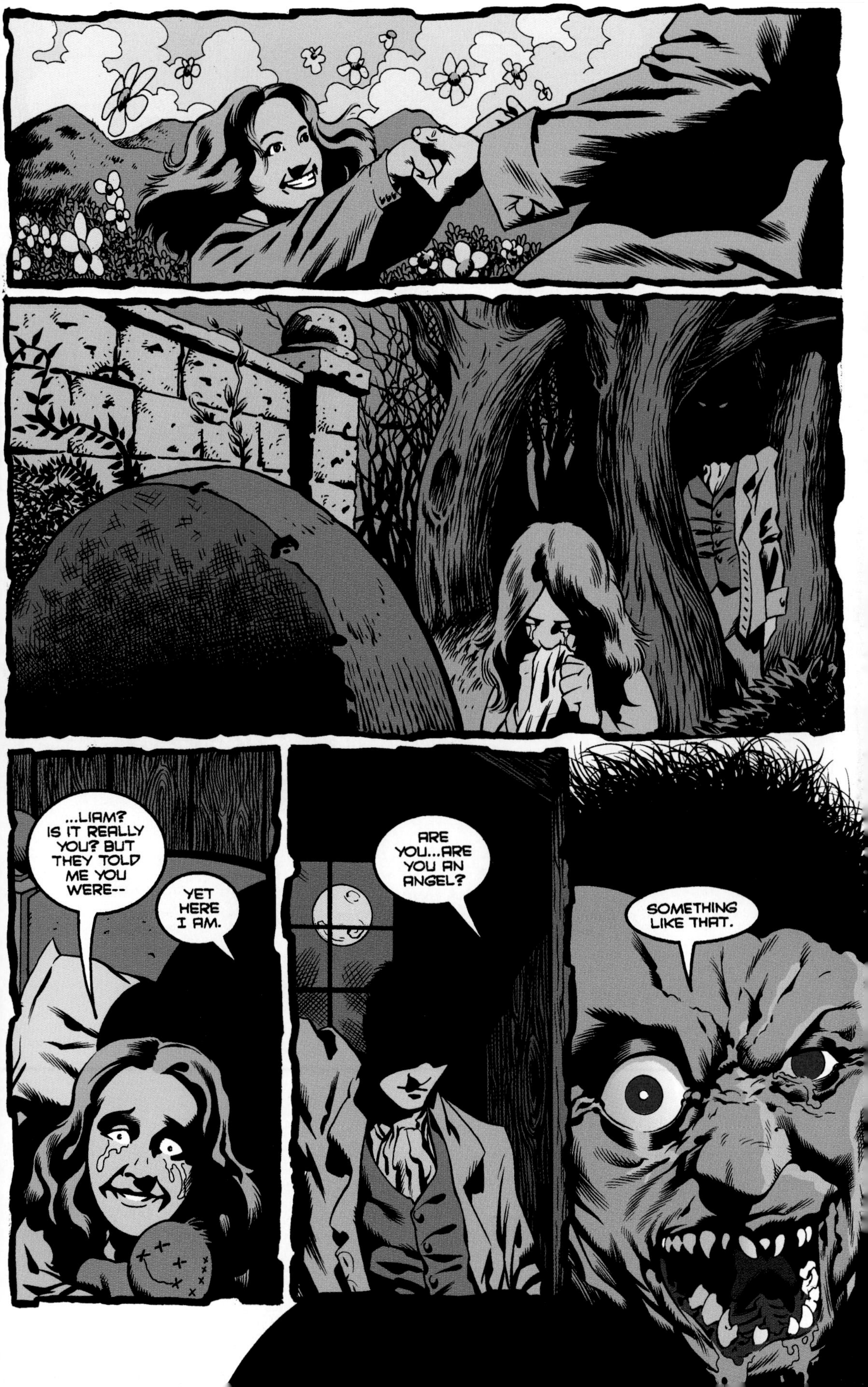
...LIAM? IS IT REALLY YOU? BUT THEY TOLD ME YOU WERE--
YET HERE I AM.
ARE YOU...ARE YOU AN ANGEL?
SOMETHING LIKE THAT.

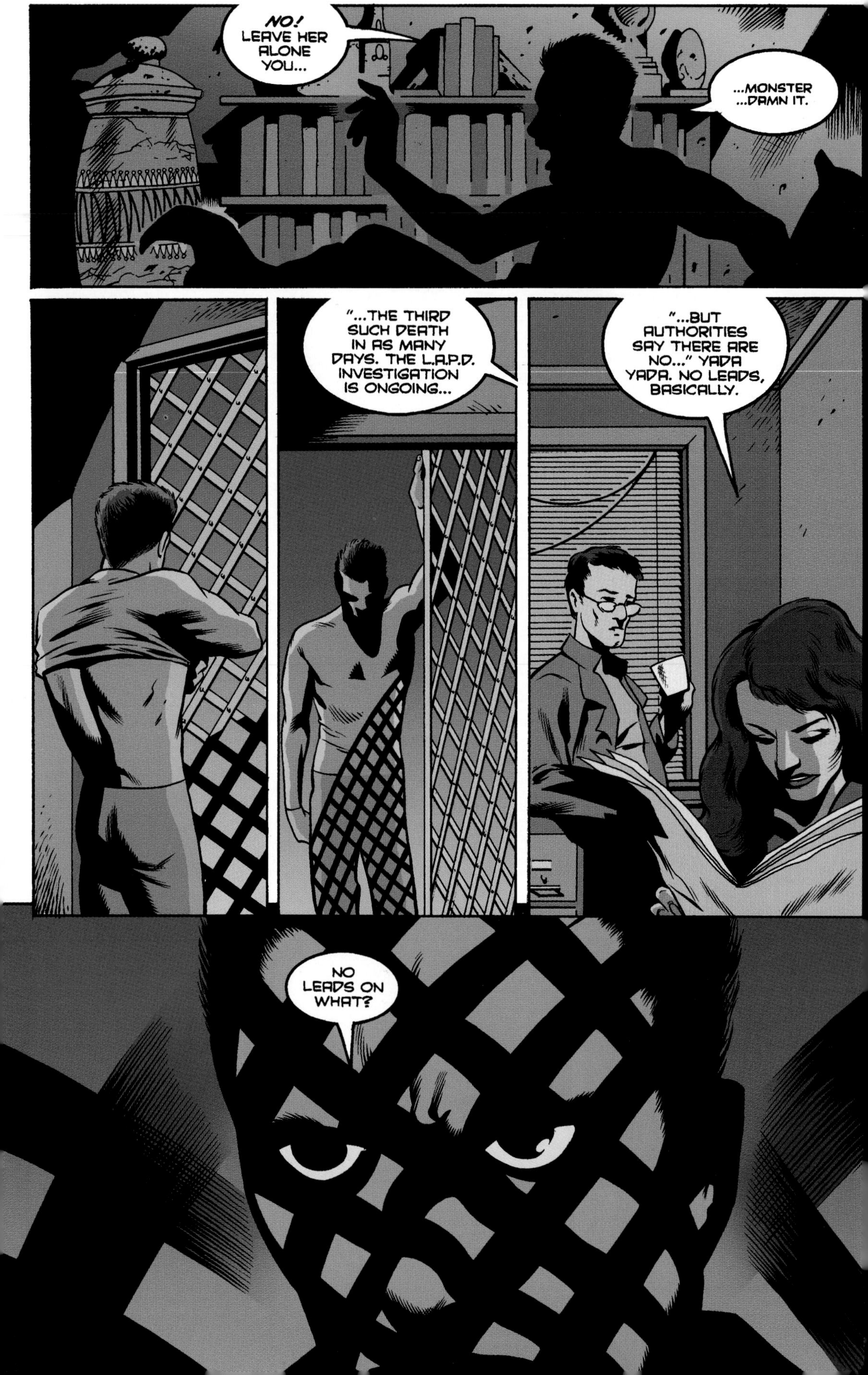
NO! LEAVE HER ALONE YOU...
...MONSTER ...DAMN IT.
"...THE THIRD SUCH DEATH IN AS MANY DAYS. THE L.A.P.D. INVESTIGATION IS ONGOING...
"...BUT AUTHORITIES SAY THERE ARE NO..." YADA YADA. NO LEADS, BASICALLY.
NO LEADS ON WHAT?

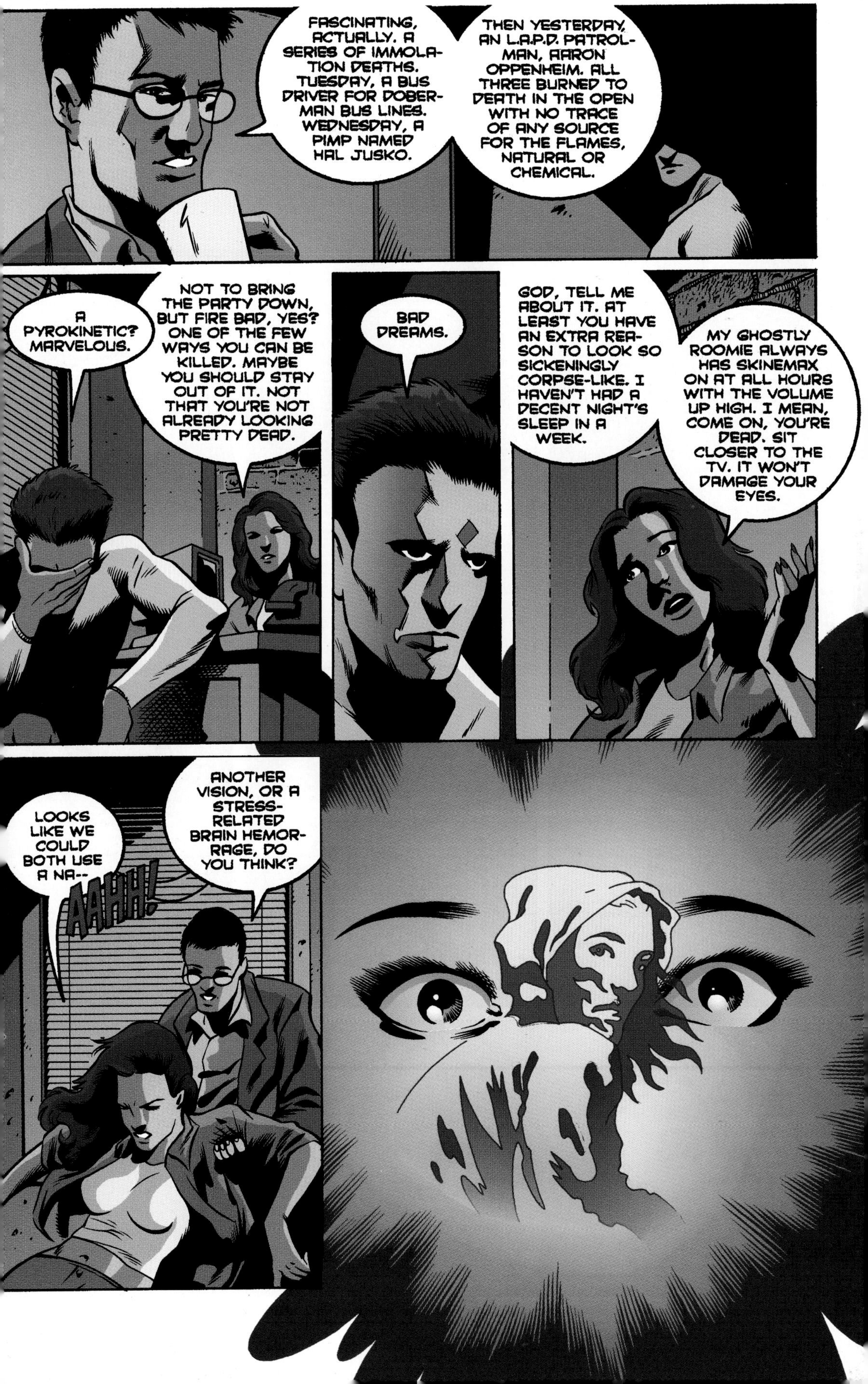
FASCINATING, ACTUALLY. A SERIES OF IMMOLATION DEATHS. TUESDAY, A BUS DRIVER FOR DOBERMAN BUS LINES. WEDNESDAY, A PIMP NAMED HAL JUSKO.
THEN YESTERDAY, AN L.A.P.D. PATROLMAN, AARON OPPENHEIM. ALL THREE BURNED TO DEATH IN THE OPEN WITH NO TRACE OF ANY SOURCE FOR THE FLAMES, NATURAL OR CHEMICAL.
A PYROKINETIC? MARVELOUS.
NOT TO BRING THE PARTY DOWN, BUT FIRE BAD, YES? ONE OF THE FEW WAYS YOU CAN BE KILLED. MAYBE YOU SHOULD STAY OUT OF IT. NOT THAT YOU'RE NOT ALREADY LOOKING PRETTY DEAD.
BAD DREAMS.
GOD, TELL ME ABOUT IT. AT LEAST YOU HAVE AN EXTRA REASON TO LOOK SO SICKENINGLY CORPSE-LIKE. I HAVEN'T HAD A DECENT NIGHT'S SLEEP IN A WEEK.
MY GHOSTLY ROOMIE ALWAYS HAS SKINEMAX ON AT ALL HOURS WITH THE VOLUME UP HIGH. I MEAN, COME ON, YOU'RE DEAD. SIT CLOSER TO THE TV. IT WON'T DAMAGE YOUR EYES.
LOOKS LIKE WE COULD BOTH USE A NA--
AAHH!
ANOTHER VISION, OR A STRESS-RELATED BRAIN HEMORRAGE, DO YOU THINK?

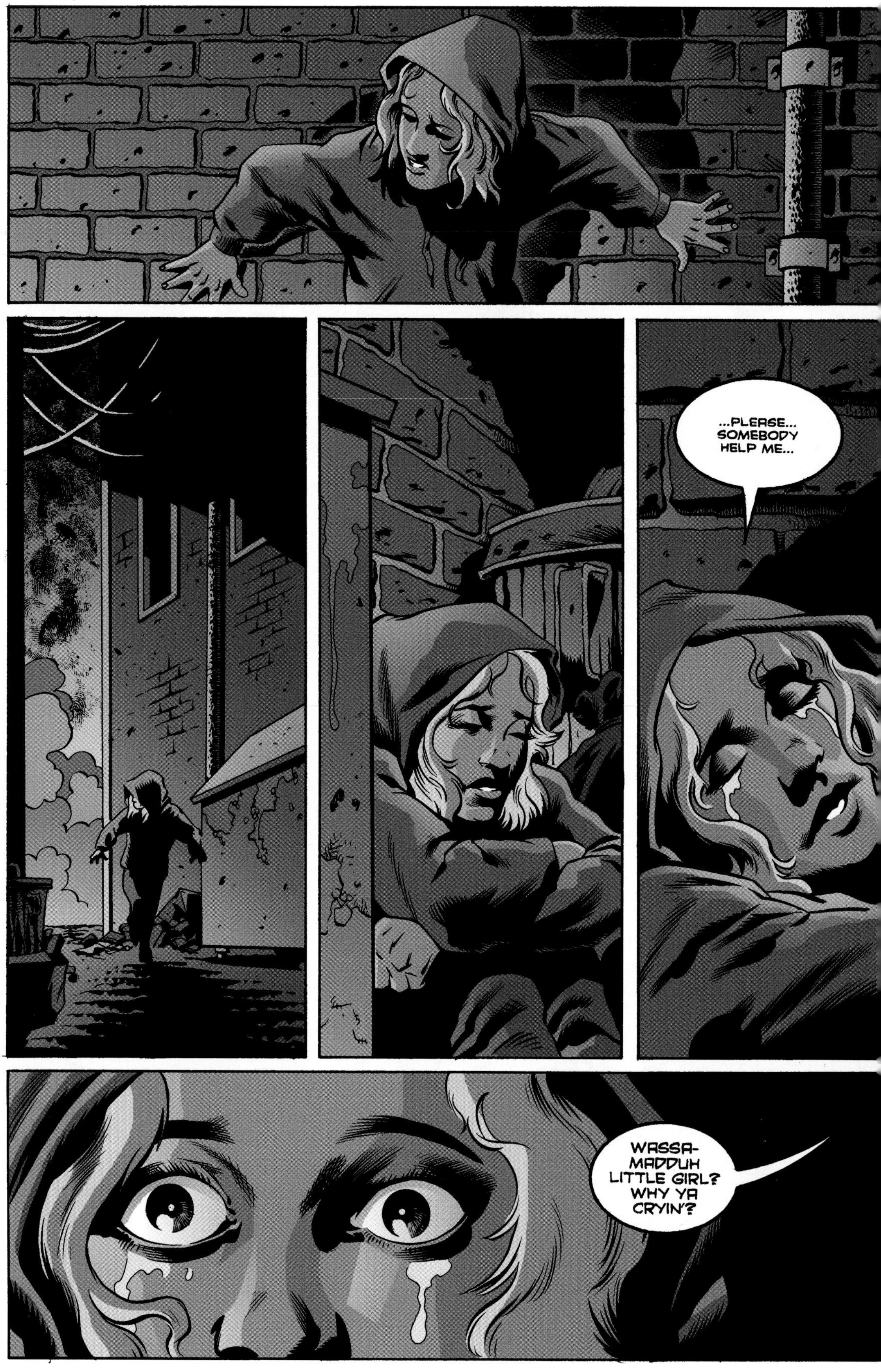
...PLEASE... SOMEBODY HELP ME...
WASSA-MADDUH LITTLE GIRL? WHY YA CRYIN'?

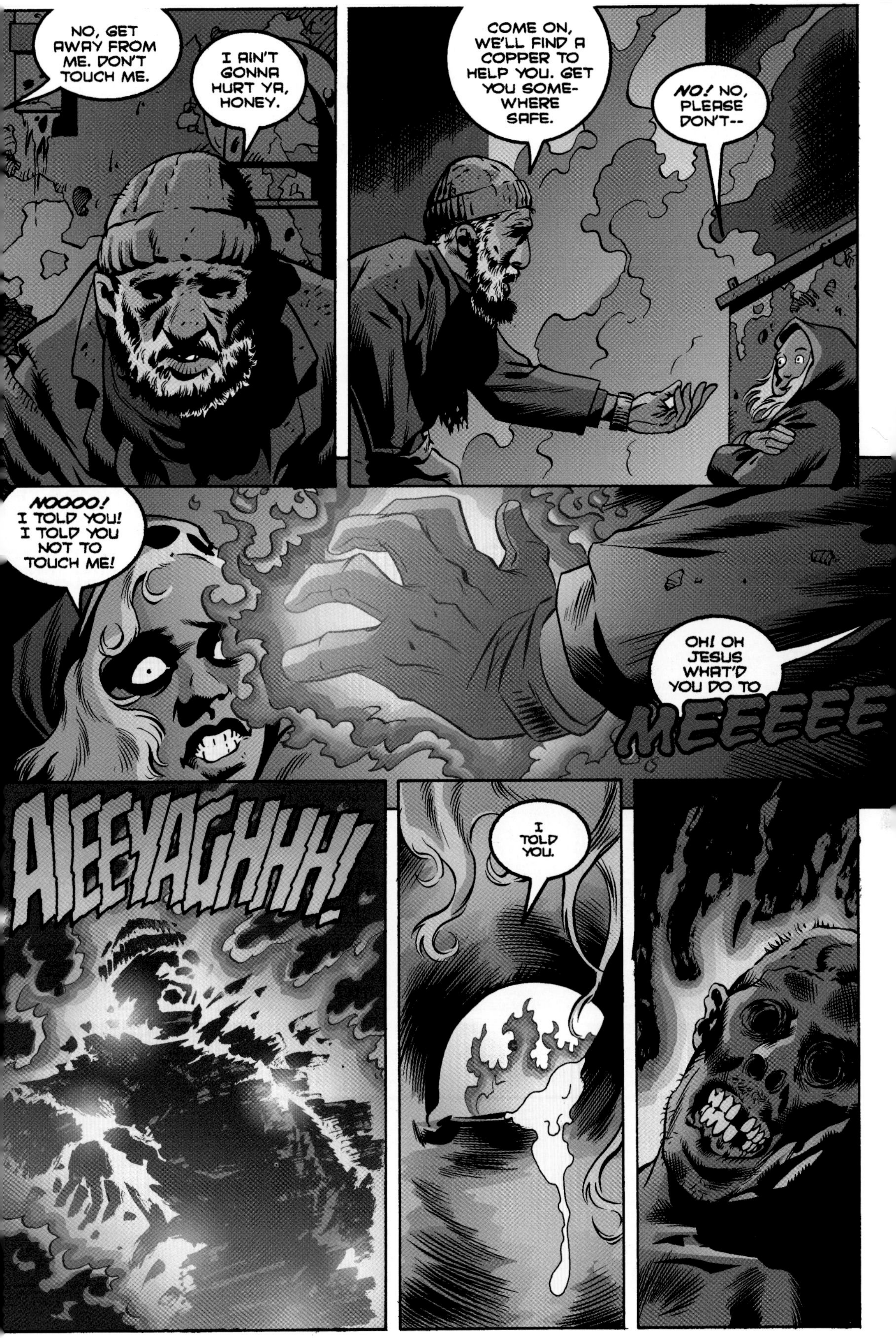

NO, GET AWAY FROM ME. DON'T TOUCH ME.
I AIN'T GONNA HURT YA, HONEY.
COME ON, WE'LL FIND A COPPER TO HELP YOU. GET YOU SOME-WHERE SAFE.
NO! NO, PLEASE DON'T--
NOOOO! I TOLD YOU! I TOLD YOU NOT TO TOUCH ME!
OH! OH JESUS WHAT'D YOU DO TO
MEEEEE
AIEEYAGHHH!
I TOLD YOU.

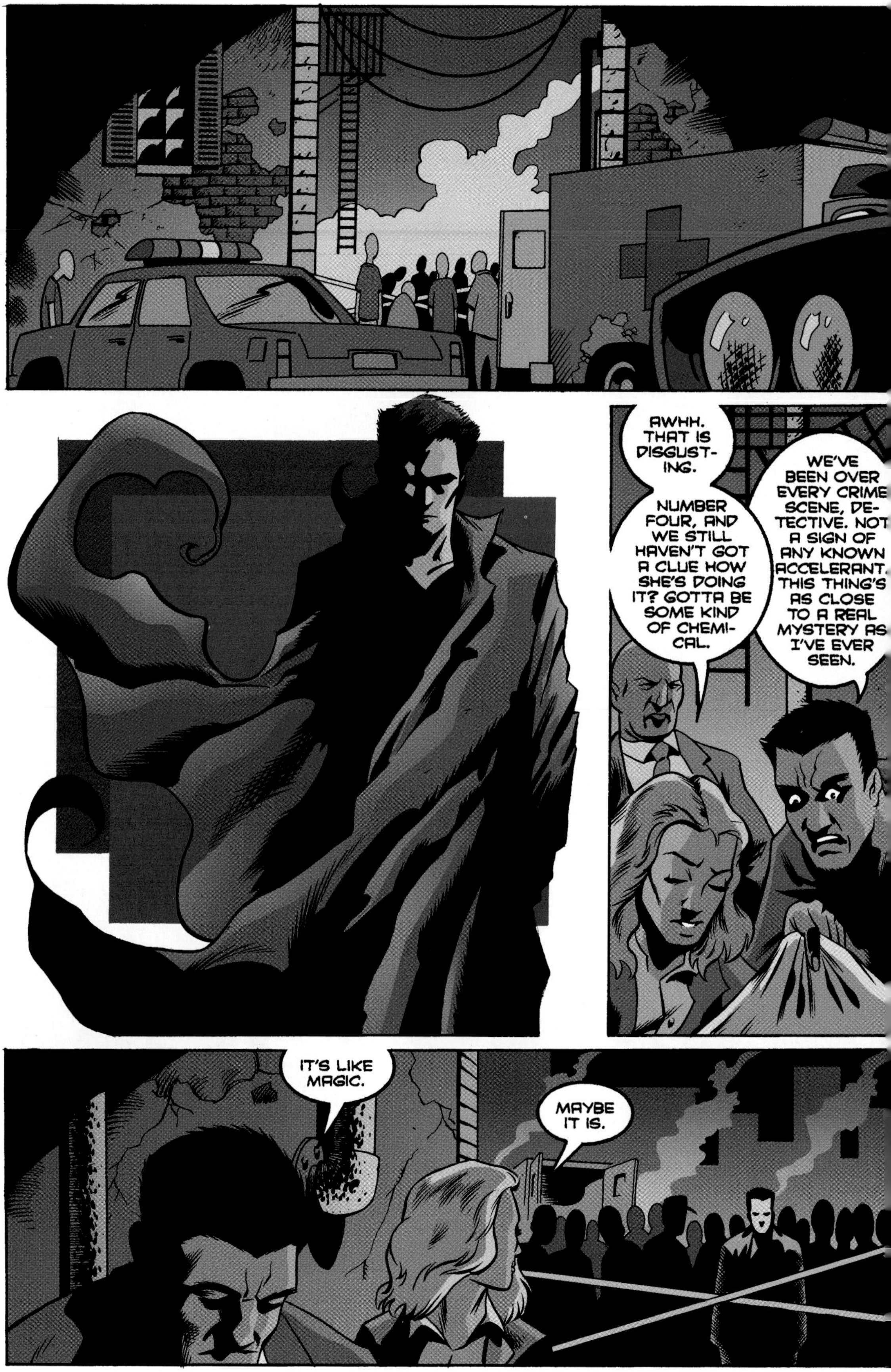

AWHH. THAT IS DISGUST-ING.
NUMBER FOUR, AND WE STILL HAVEN'T GOT A CLUE HOW SHE'S DOING IT? GOTTA BE SOME KIND OF CHEMI-CAL.
WE'VE BEEN OVER EVERY CRIME SCENE, DE-TECTIVE. NOT A SIGN OF ANY KNOWN ACCELERANT. THIS THING'S AS CLOSE TO A REAL MYSTERY AS I'VE EVER SEEN.
IT'S LIKE MAGIC.
MAYBE IT IS.

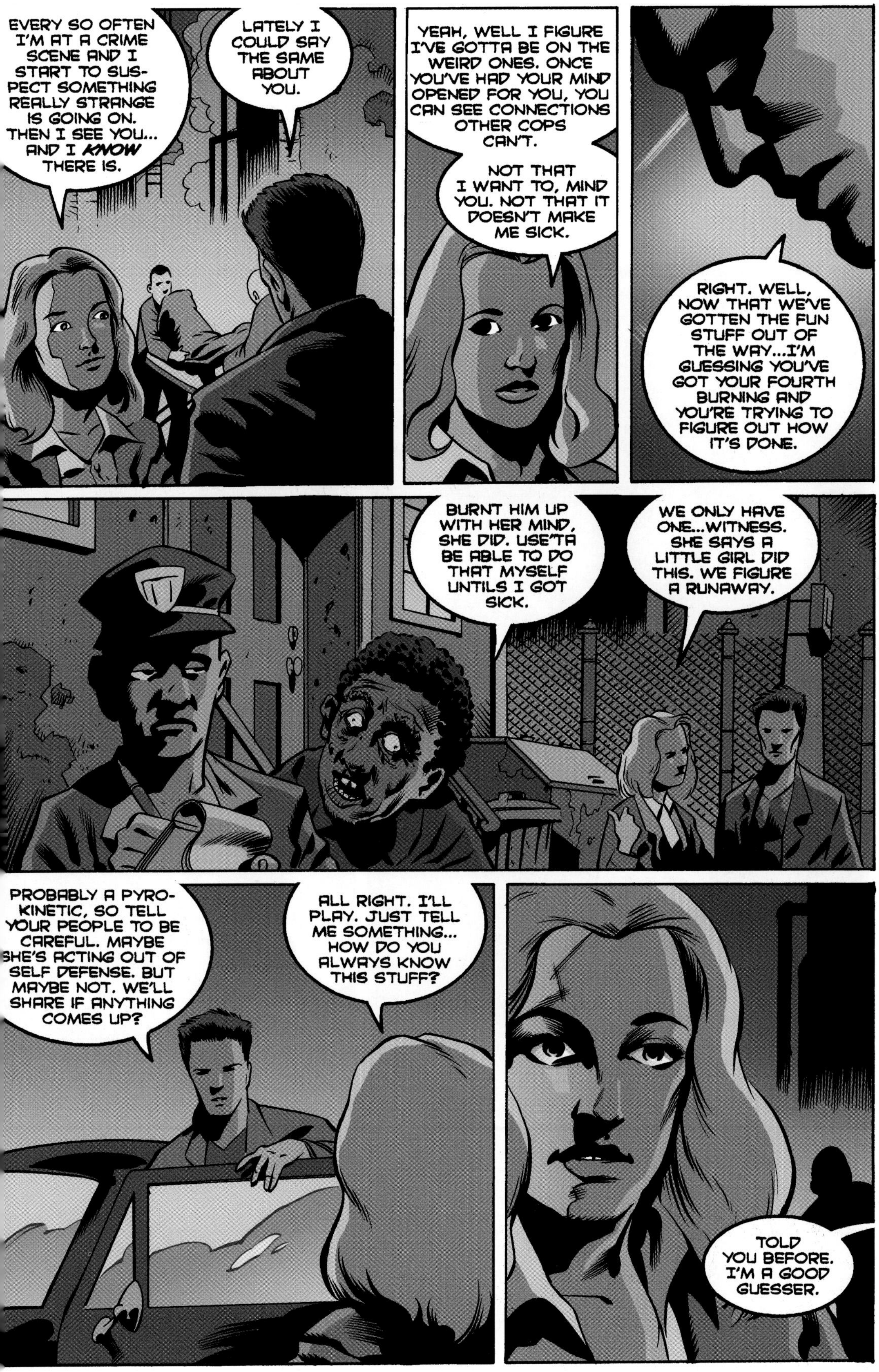
EVERY SO OFTEN I'M AT A CRIME SCENE AND I START TO SUS-PECT SOMETHING REALLY STRANGE IS GOING ON. THEN I SEE YOU... AND I *KNOW* THERE IS.
LATELY I COULD SAY THE SAME ABOUT YOU.
YEAH, WELL I FIGURE I'VE GOTTA BE ON THE WEIRD ONES. ONCE YOU'VE HAD YOUR MIND OPENED FOR YOU, YOU CAN SEE CONNECTIONS OTHER COPS CAN'T.
NOT THAT I WANT TO, MIND YOU. NOT THAT IT DOESN'T MAKE ME SICK.
RIGHT. WELL, NOW THAT WE'VE GOTTEN THE FUN STUFF OUT OF THE WAY...I'M GUESSING YOU'VE GOT YOUR FOURTH BURNING AND YOU'RE TRYING TO FIGURE OUT HOW IT'S DONE.
BURNT HIM UP WITH HER MIND, SHE DID. USE'TA BE ABLE TO DO THAT MYSELF UNTILS I GOT SICK.
WE ONLY HAVE ONE...WITNESS. SHE SAYS A LITTLE GIRL DID THIS. WE FIGURE A RUNAWAY.
PROBABLY A PYRO-KINETIC, SO TELL YOUR PEOPLE TO BE CAREFUL. MAYBE SHE'S ACTING OUT OF SELF DEFENSE. BUT MAYBE NOT. WE'LL SHARE IF ANYTHING COMES UP?
ALL RIGHT. I'LL PLAY. JUST TELL ME SOMETHING... HOW DO YOU ALWAYS KNOW THIS STUFF?
TOLD YOU BEFORE. I'M A GOOD GUESSER.

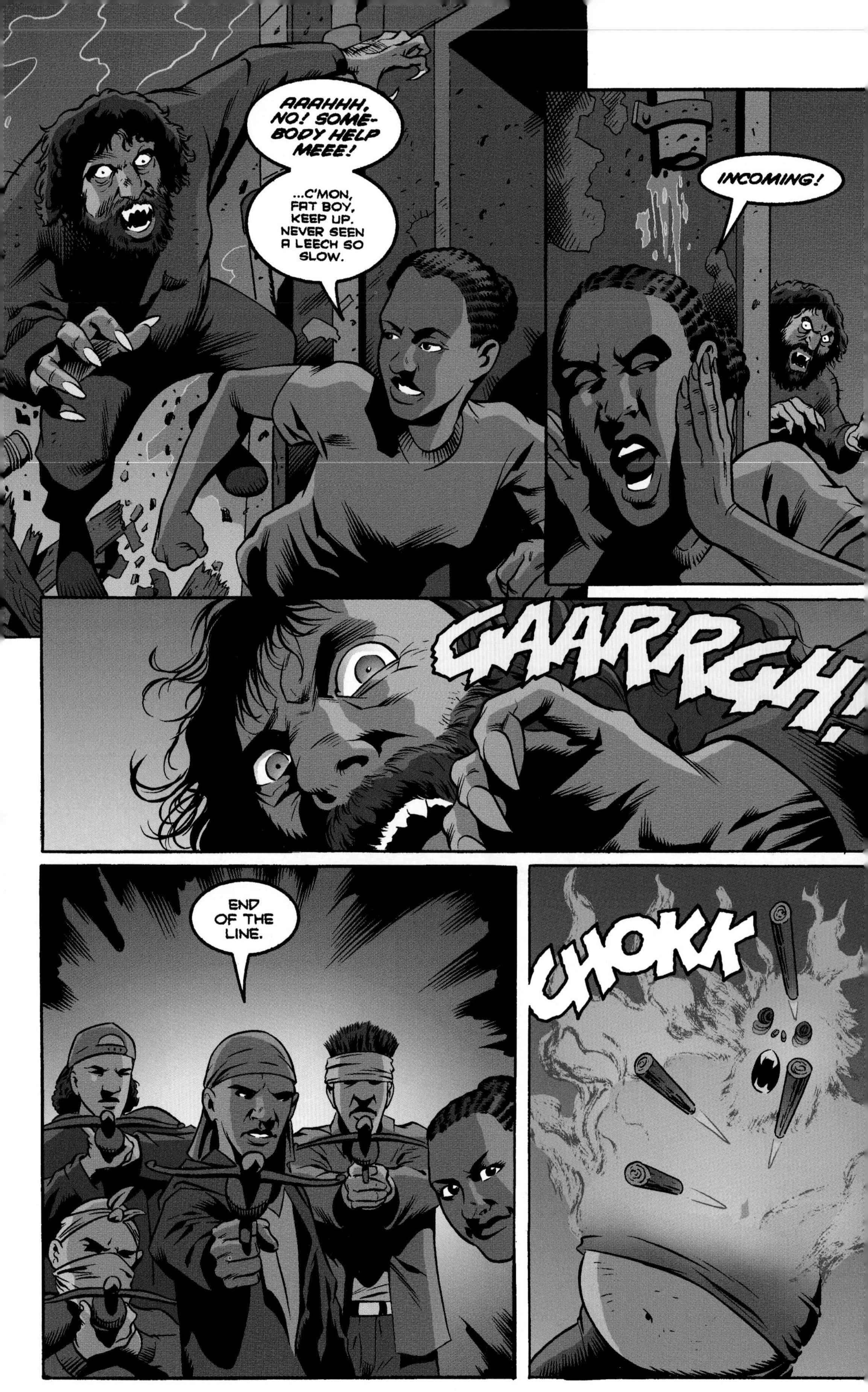
ARAHHH, NO! SOME-BODY HELP MEEE!
...C'MON, FAT BOY, KEEP UP. NEVER SEEN A LEECH SO SLOW.
INCOMING!
GAARRGH!
END OF THE LINE.
CHOKK

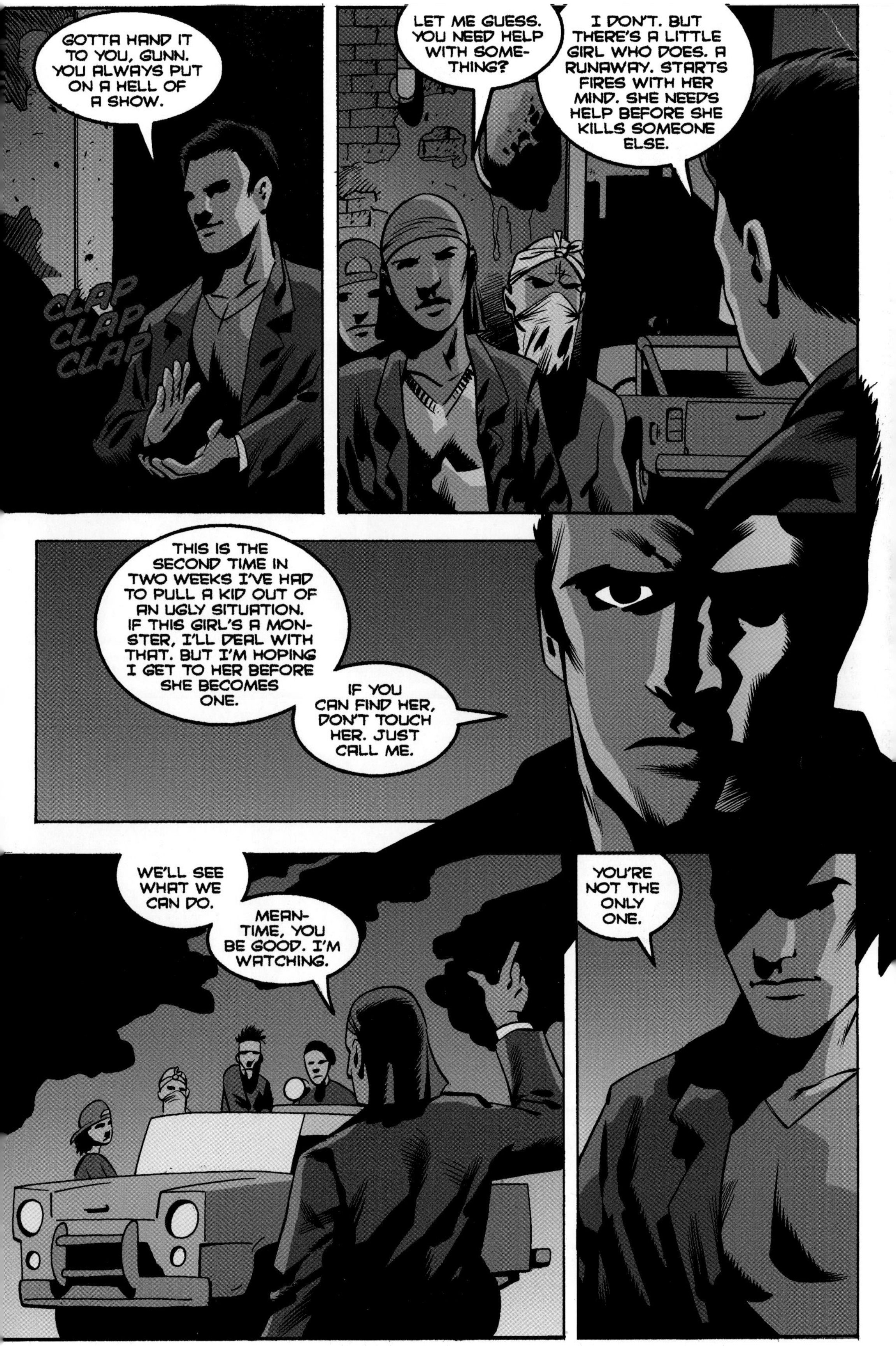
GOTTA HAND IT TO YOU, GUNN. YOU ALWAYS PUT ON A HELL OF A SHOW.
CLAP CLAP CLAP
LET ME GUESS. YOU NEED HELP WITH SOME-THING?
I DON'T. BUT THERE'S A LITTLE GIRL WHO DOES. A RUNAWAY. STARTS FIRES WITH HER MIND. SHE NEEDS HELP BEFORE SHE KILLS SOMEONE ELSE.
THIS IS THE SECOND TIME IN TWO WEEKS I'VE HAD TO PULL A KID OUT OF AN UGLY SITUATION. IF THIS GIRL'S A MON-STER, I'LL DEAL WITH THAT. BUT I'M HOPING I GET TO HER BEFORE SHE BECOMES ONE.
IF YOU CAN FIND HER, DON'T TOUCH HER. JUST CALL ME.
WE'LL SEE WHAT WE CAN DO.
MEAN-TIME, YOU BE GOOD. I'M WATCHING.
YOU'RE NOT THE ONLY ONE.

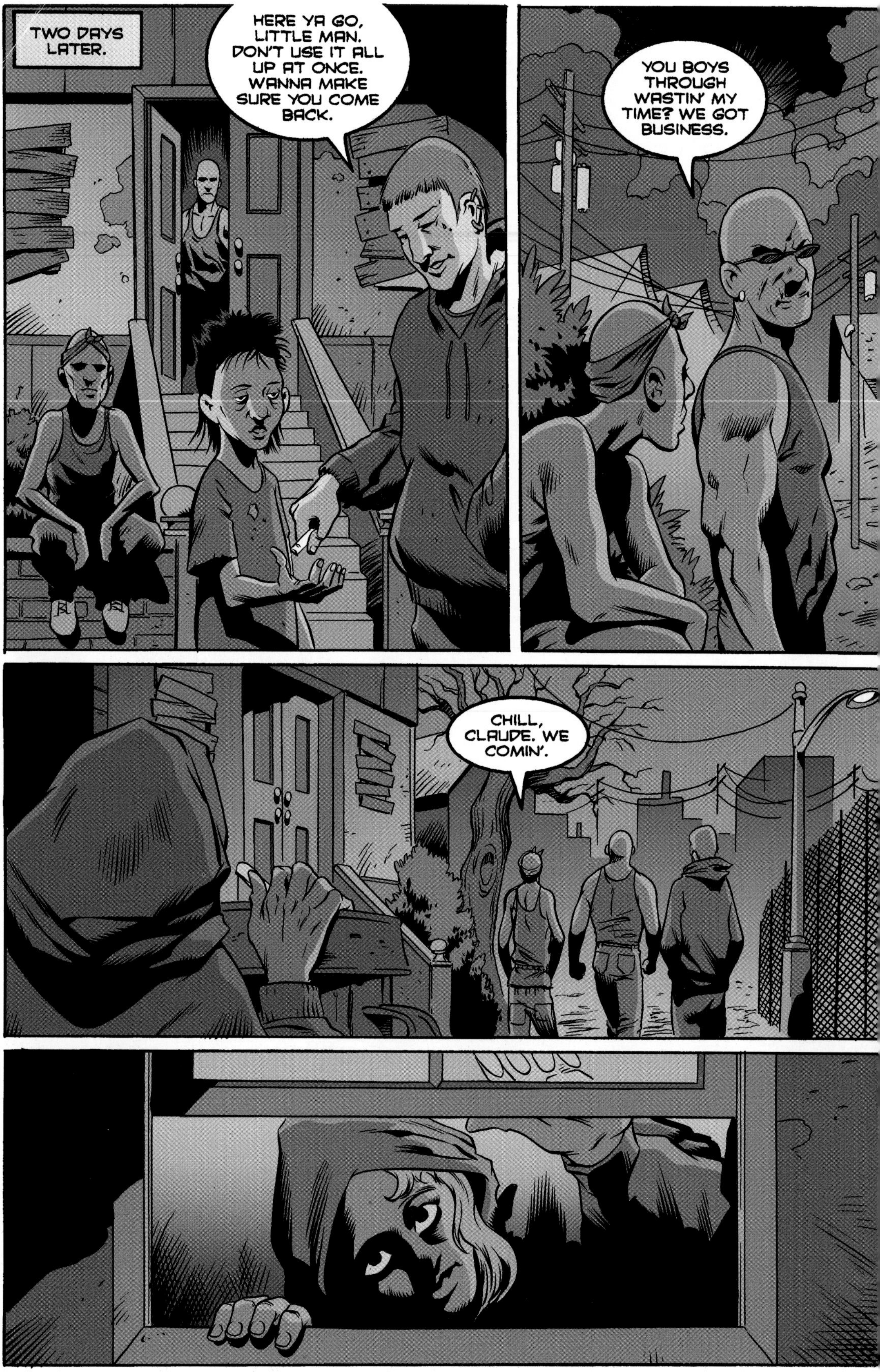
TWO DAYS LATER.
HERE YA GO, LITTLE MAN. DON'T USE IT ALL UP AT ONCE. WANNA MAKE SURE YOU COME BACK.
YOU BOYS THROUGH WASTIN' MY TIME? WE GOT BUSINESS.
CHILL, CLAUDE. WE COMIN'.

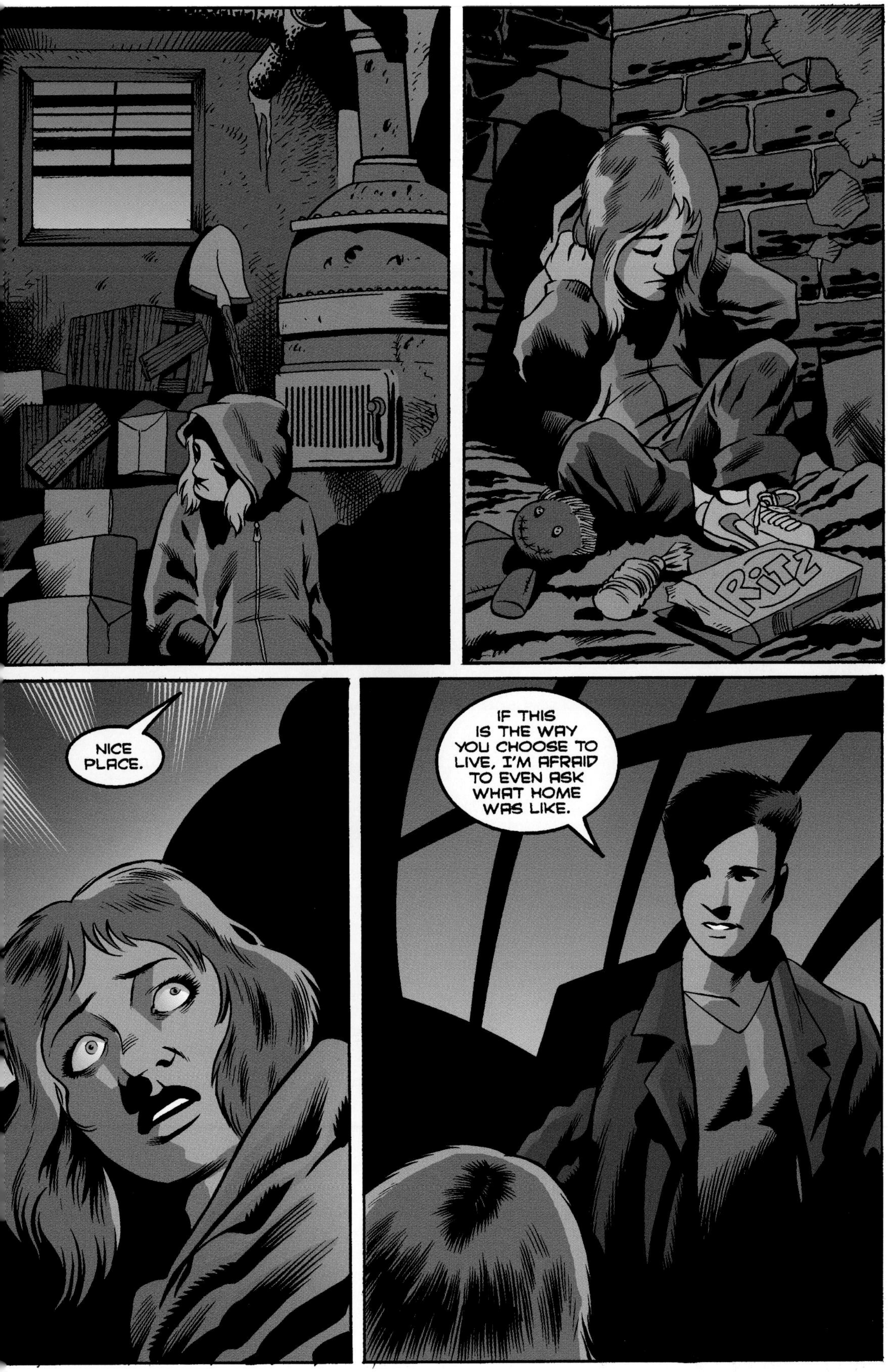

RiTZ
NICE PLACE.
IF THIS IS THE WAY YOU CHOOSE TO LIVE, I'M AFRAID TO EVEN ASK WHAT HOME WAS LIKE.

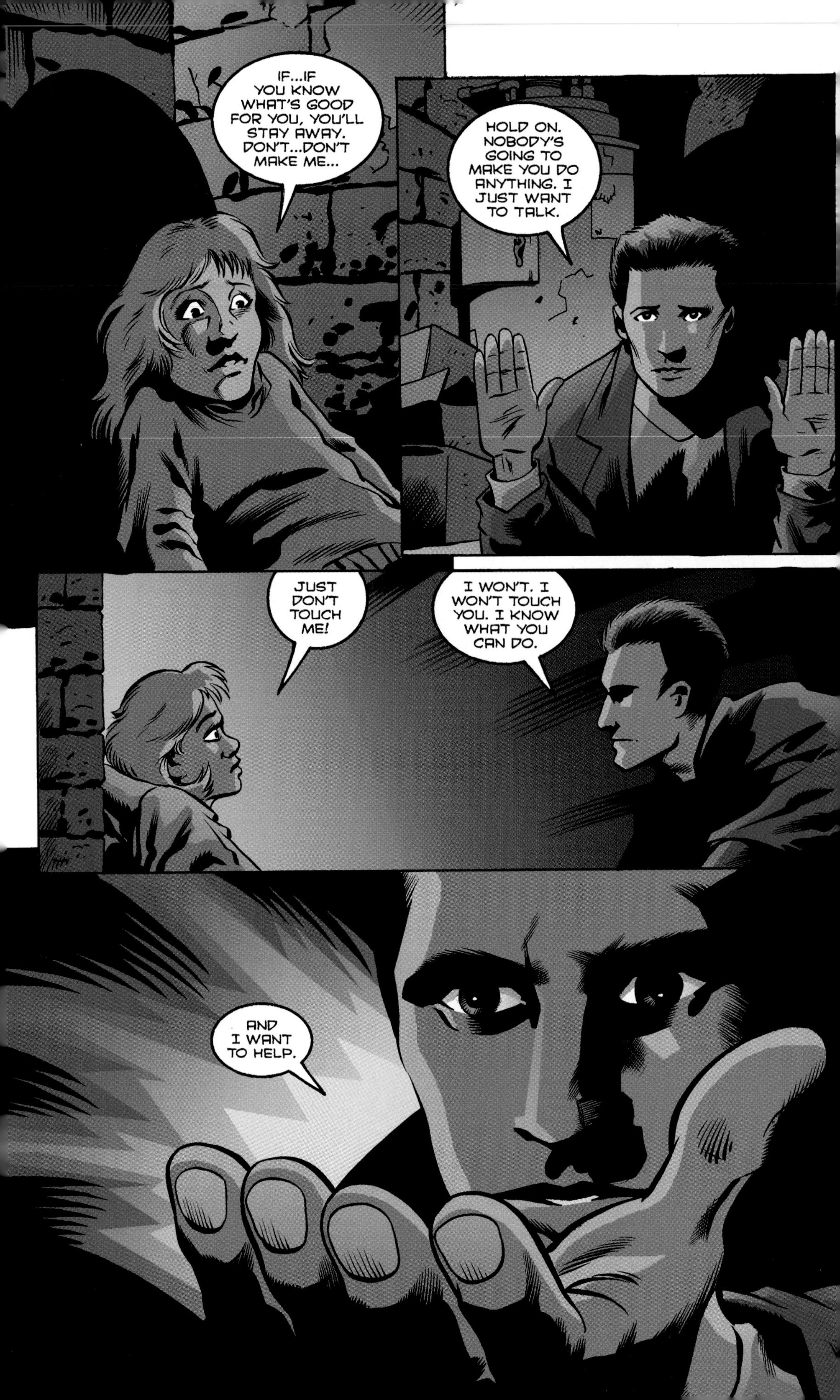
IF...IF YOU KNOW WHAT'S GOOD FOR YOU, YOU'LL STAY AWAY. DON'T...DON'T MAKE ME...
HOLD ON. NOBODY'S GOING TO MAKE YOU DO ANYTHING. I JUST WANT TO TALK.
JUST DON'T TOUCH ME!
I WON'T. I WON'T TOUCH YOU. I KNOW WHAT YOU CAN DO.
AND I WANT TO HELP.

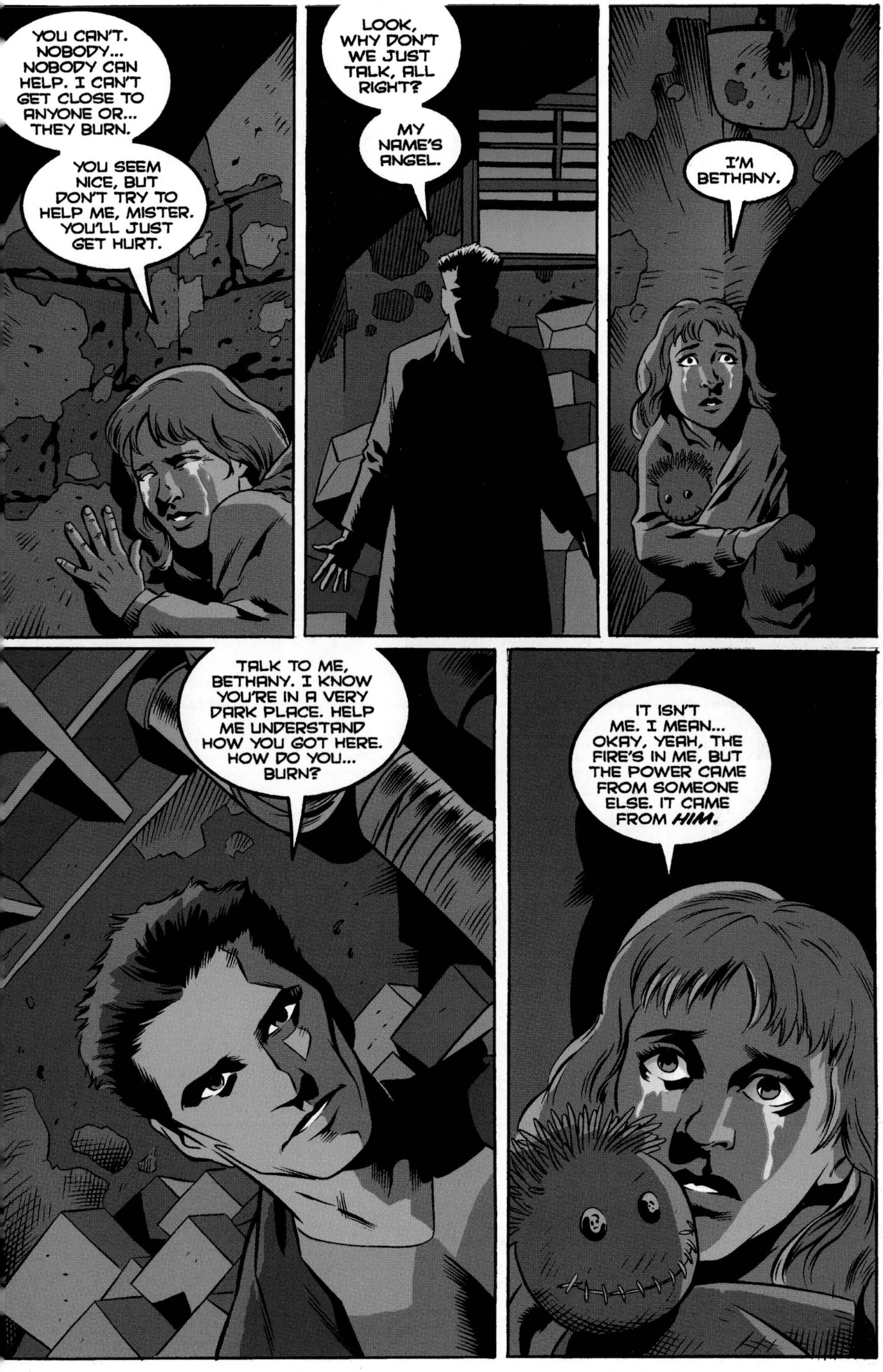

YOU CAN'T. NOBODY... NOBODY CAN HELP. I CAN'T GET CLOSE TO ANYONE OR... THEY BURN.
YOU SEEM NICE, BUT DON'T TRY TO HELP ME, MISTER. YOU'LL JUST GET HURT.
LOOK, WHY DON'T WE JUST TALK, ALL RIGHT?
MY NAME'S ANGEL.
I'M BETHANY.
TALK TO ME, BETHANY. I KNOW YOU'RE IN A VERY DARK PLACE. HELP ME UNDERSTAND HOW YOU GOT HERE. HOW DO YOU... BURN?
IT ISN'T ME. I MEAN... OKAY, YEAH, THE FIRE'S IN ME, BUT THE POWER CAME FROM SOMEONE ELSE. IT CAME FROM *HIM*.

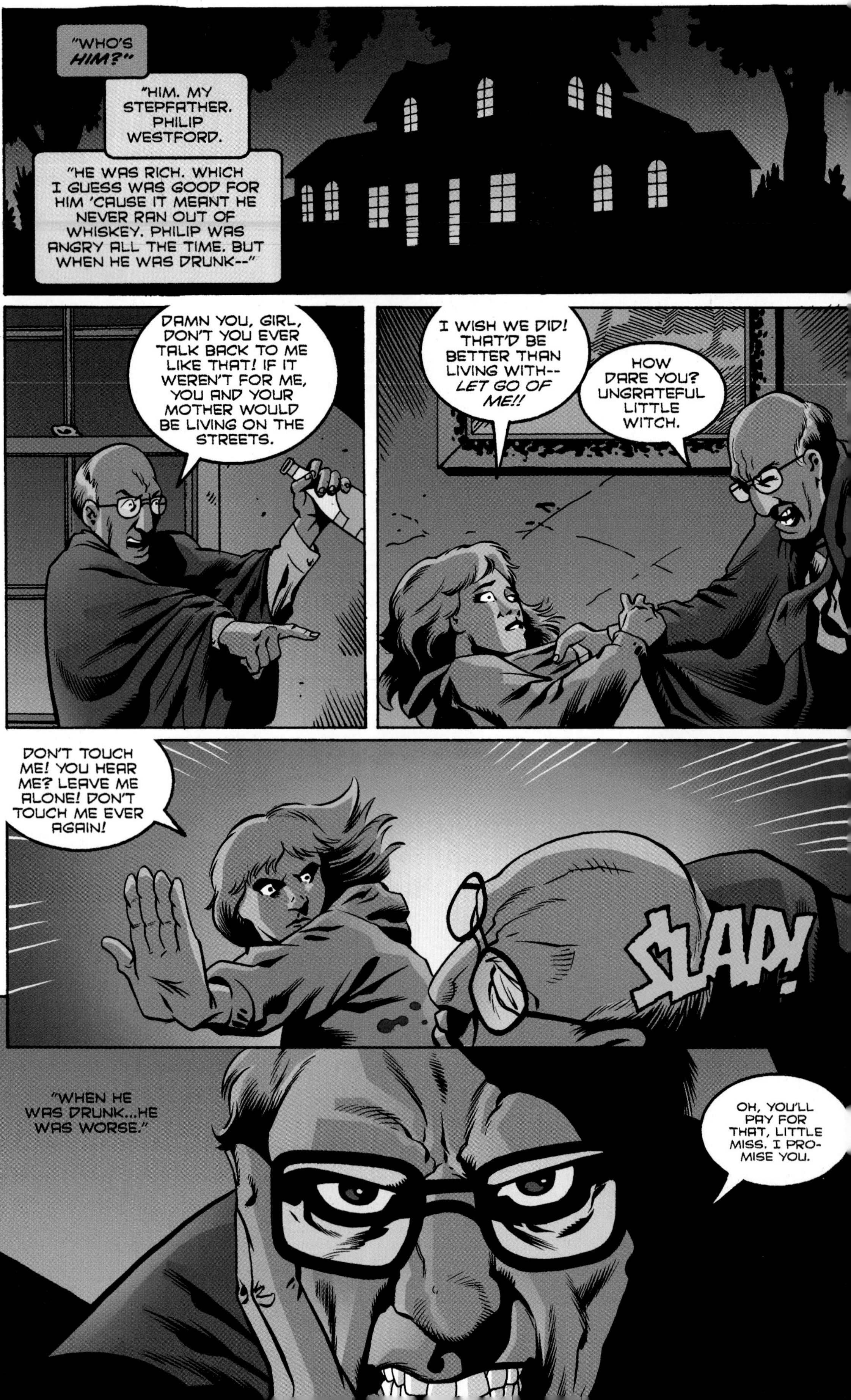
"WHO'S *HIM?*"
"HIM. MY STEPFATHER. PHILIP WESTFORD.
"HE WAS RICH. WHICH I GUESS WAS GOOD FOR HIM 'CAUSE IT MEANT HE NEVER RAN OUT OF WHISKEY. PHILIP WAS ANGRY ALL THE TIME. BUT WHEN HE WAS DRUNK--"
DAMN YOU, GIRL, DON'T YOU EVER TALK BACK TO ME LIKE THAT! IF IT WEREN'T FOR ME, YOU AND YOUR MOTHER WOULD BE LIVING ON THE STREETS.
I WISH WE DID! THAT'D BE BETTER THAN LIVING WITH-- *LET GO OF ME!!*
HOW DARE YOU? UNGRATEFUL LITTLE WITCH.
DON'T TOUCH ME! YOU HEAR ME? LEAVE ME ALONE! DON'T TOUCH ME EVER AGAIN!
SLAP!
"WHEN HE WAS DRUNK...HE WAS WORSE."
OH, YOU'LL PAY FOR THAT, LITTLE MISS. I PRO-MISE YOU.

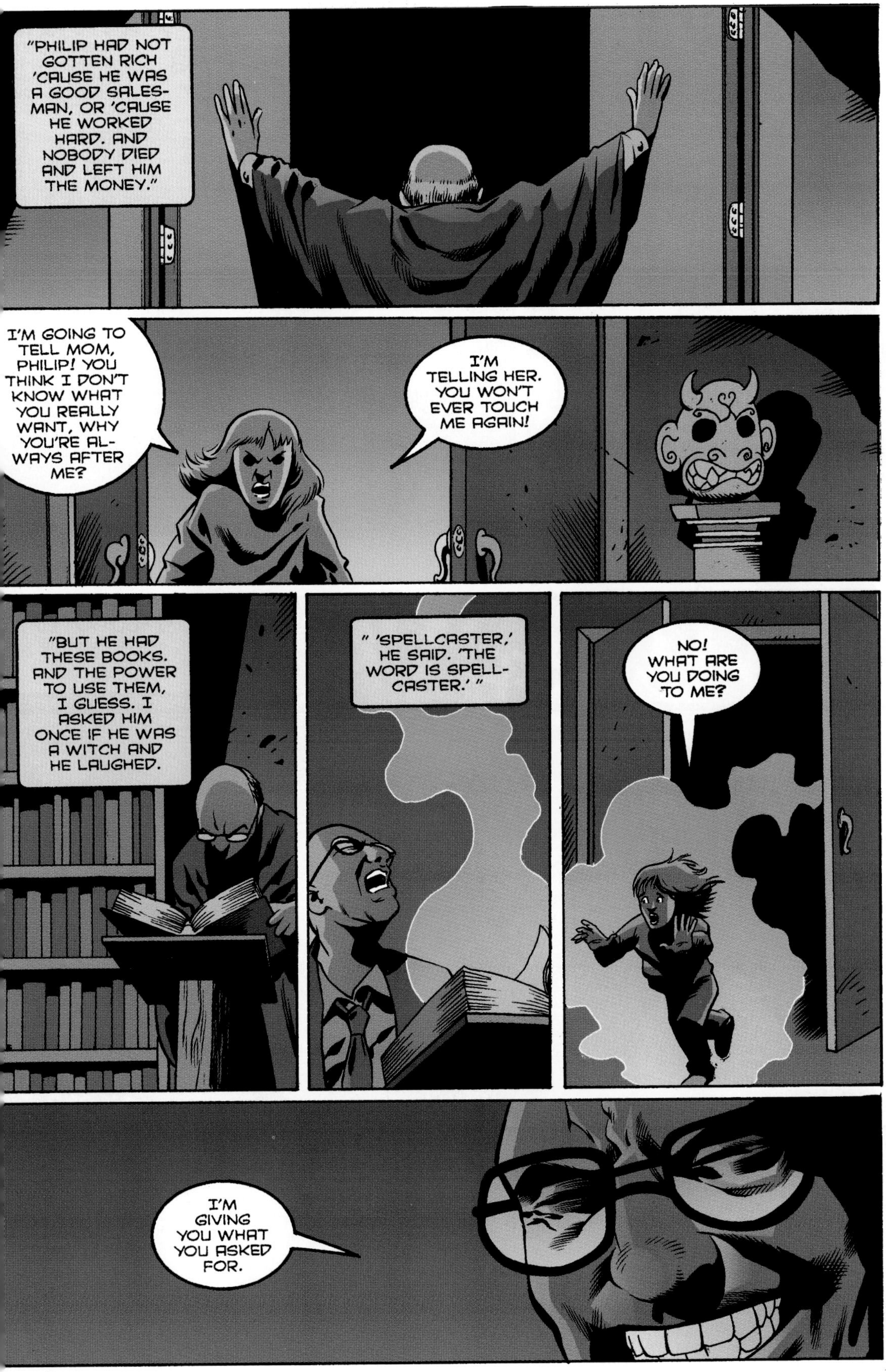
"PHILIP HAD NOT GOTTEN RICH 'CAUSE HE WAS A GOOD SALES-MAN, OR 'CAUSE HE WORKED HARD. AND NOBODY DIED AND LEFT HIM THE MONEY."
I'M GOING TO TELL MOM, PHILIP! YOU THINK I DON'T KNOW WHAT YOU REALLY WANT, WHY YOU'RE AL-WAYS AFTER ME?
I'M TELLING HER. YOU WON'T EVER TOUCH ME AGAIN!
"BUT HE HAD THESE BOOKS. AND THE POWER TO USE THEM, I GUESS. I ASKED HIM ONCE IF HE WAS A WITCH AND HE LAUGHED.
" 'SPELLCASTER,' HE SAID. 'THE WORD IS SPELL-CASTER.' "
NO! WHAT ARE YOU DOING TO ME?
I'M GIVING YOU WHAT YOU ASKED FOR.

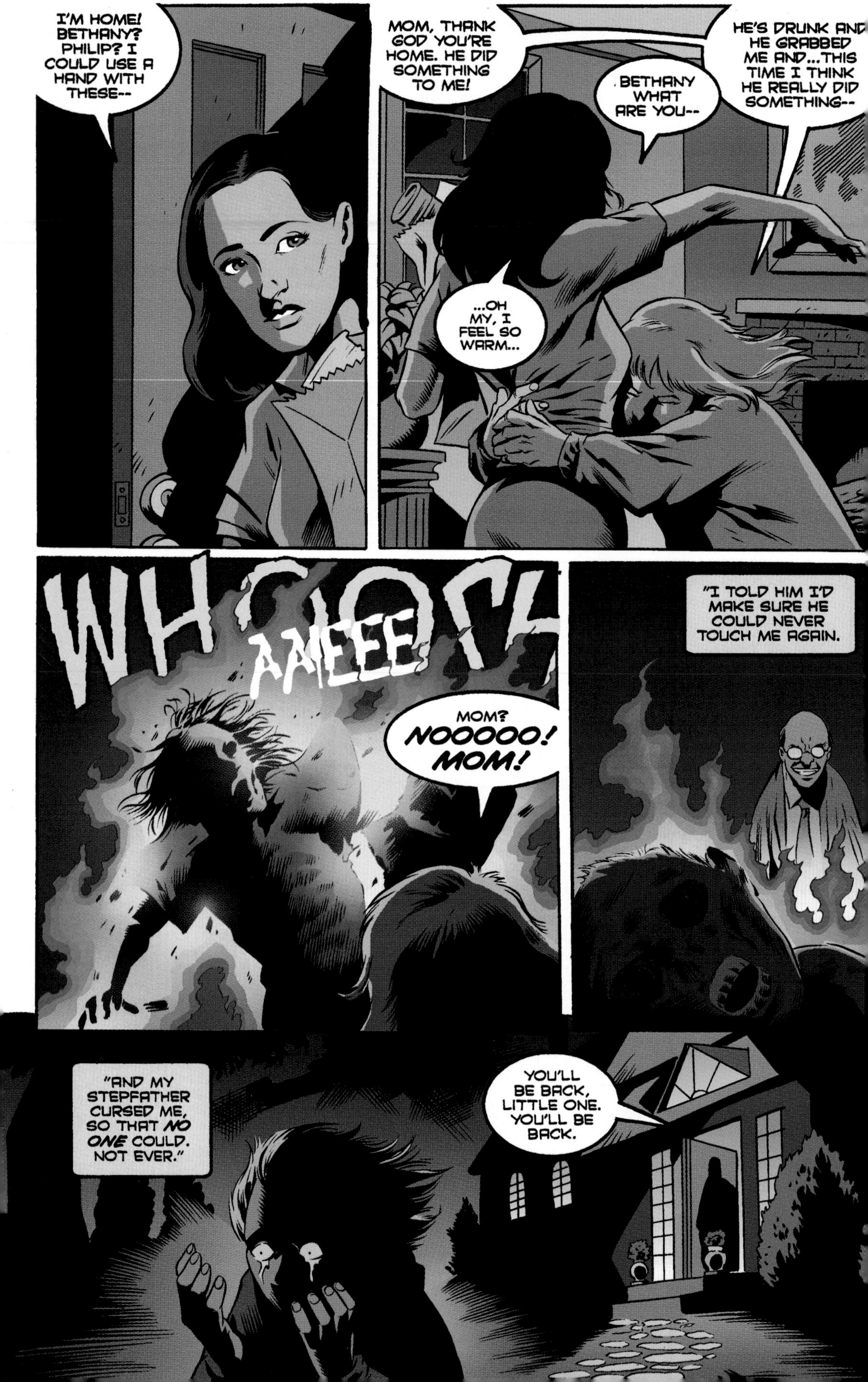
I'M HOME! BETHANY? PHILIP? I COULD USE A HAND WITH THESE--
MOM, THANK GOD YOU'RE HOME. HE DID SOMETHING TO ME!
BETHANY WHAT ARE YOU--
HE'S DRUNK AND HE GRABBED ME AND...THIS TIME I THINK HE REALLY DID SOMETHING--
...OH MY, I FEEL SO WARM...
WHOOSH
AAIEEE
MOM? NOOOOO! MOM!
"I TOLD HIM I'D MAKE SURE HE COULD NEVER TOUCH ME AGAIN.
"AND MY STEPFATHER CURSED ME, SO THAT NO ONE COULD. NOT EVER."
YOU'LL BE BACK, LITTLE ONE. YOU'LL BE BACK.

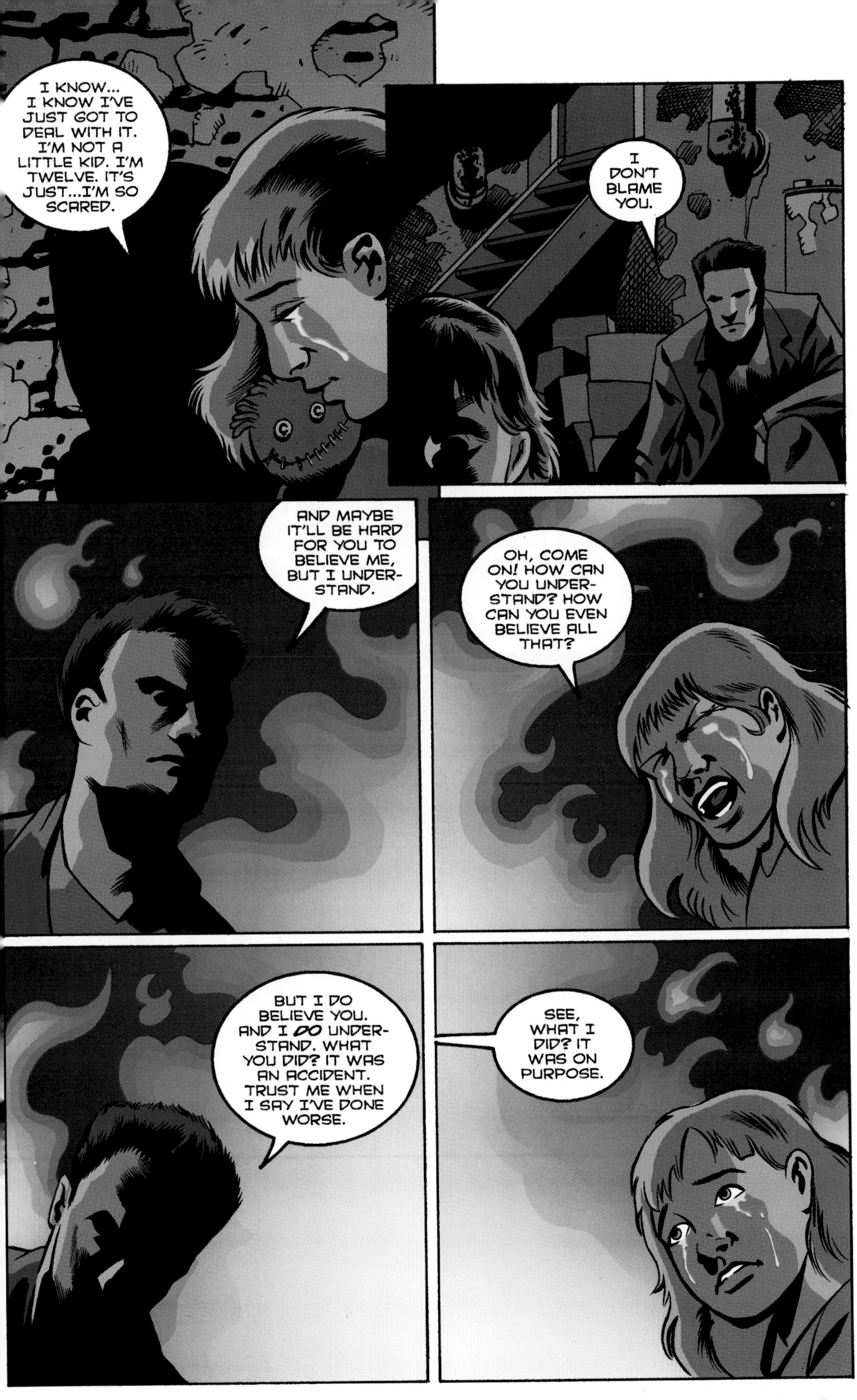
I KNOW... I KNOW I'VE JUST GOT TO DEAL WITH IT. I'M NOT A LITTLE KID. I'M TWELVE. IT'S JUST...I'M SO SCARED.
I DON'T BLAME YOU.
AND MAYBE IT'LL BE HARD FOR YOU TO BELIEVE ME, BUT I UNDER-STAND.
OH, COME ON! HOW CAN YOU UNDER-STAND? HOW CAN YOU EVEN BELIEVE ALL THAT?
BUT I DO BELIEVE YOU. AND I *DO* UNDER-STAND. WHAT YOU DID? IT WAS AN ACCIDENT. TRUST ME WHEN I SAY I'VE DONE WORSE.
SEE, WHAT I DID? IT WAS ON PURPOSE.

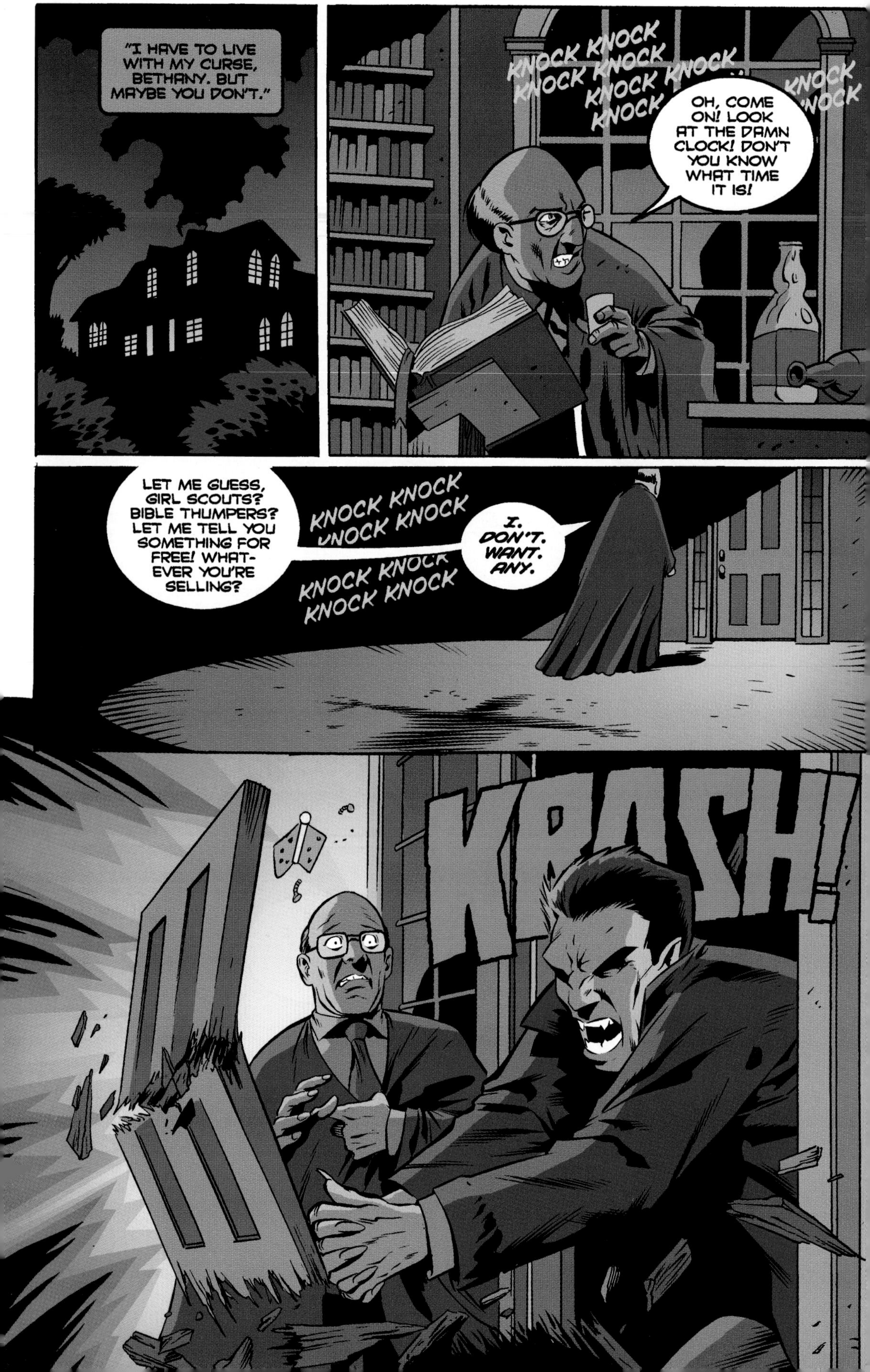
"I HAVE TO LIVE WITH MY CURSE, BETHANY. BUT MAYBE YOU DON'T."
KNOCK KNOCK KNOCK KNOCK KNOCK KNOCK KNOCK KNOCK
OH, COME ON! LOOK AT THE DAMN CLOCK! DON'T YOU KNOW WHAT TIME IT IS!
KNOCK KNOCK
LET ME GUESS, GIRL SCOUTS? BIBLE THUMPERS? LET ME TELL YOU SOMETHING FOR FREE! WHATEVER YOU'RE SELLING?
KNOCK KNOCK KNOCK KNOCK
KNOCK KNOCK KNOCK KNOCK
I. DON'T. WANT. ANY.
KRASH!

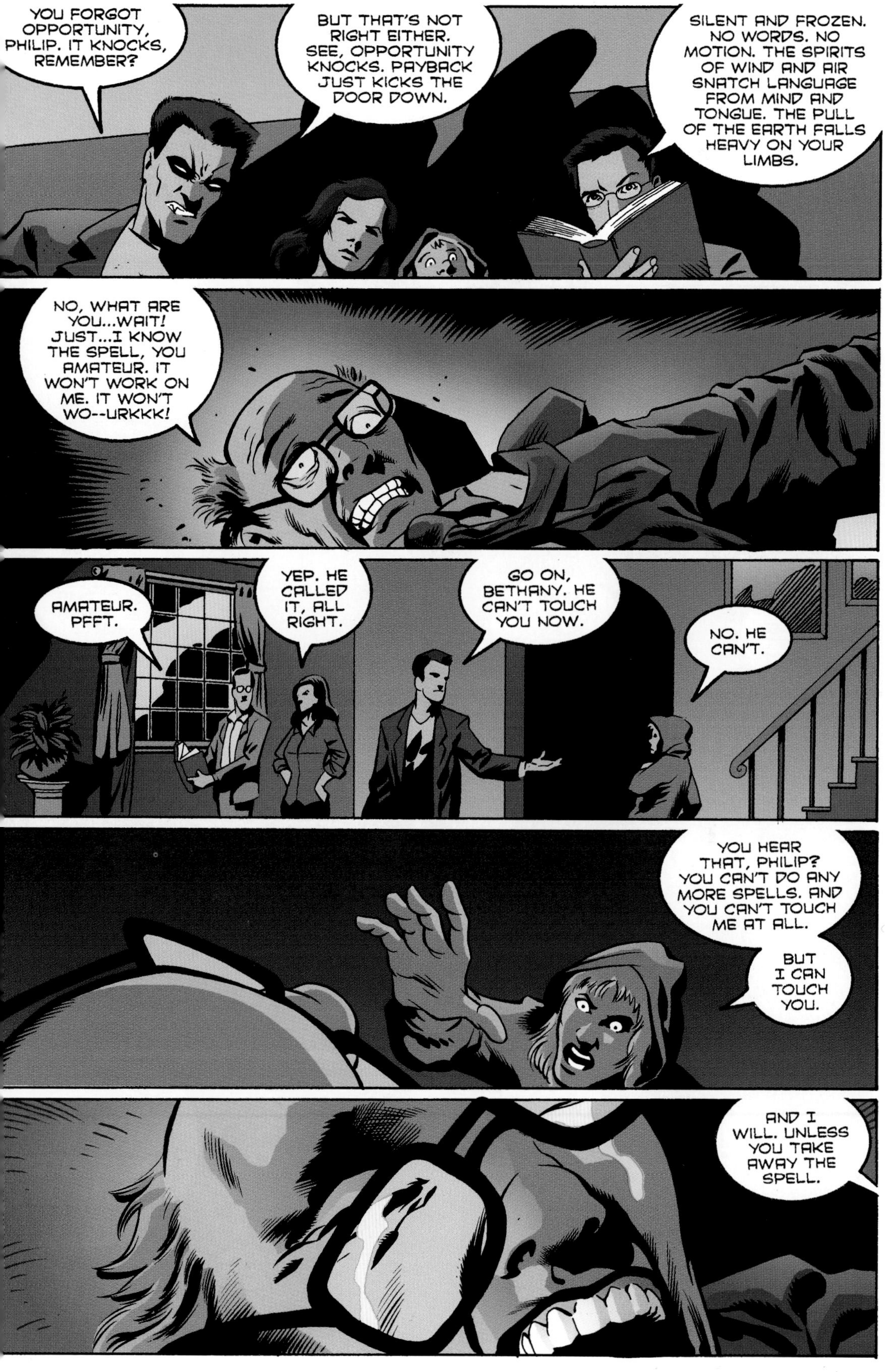
YOU FORGOT OPPORTUNITY, PHILIP. IT KNOCKS, REMEMBER?
BUT THAT'S NOT RIGHT EITHER. SEE, OPPORTUNITY KNOCKS. PAYBACK JUST KICKS THE DOOR DOWN.
SILENT AND FROZEN. NO WORDS. NO MOTION. THE SPIRITS OF WIND AND AIR SNATCH LANGUAGE FROM MIND AND TONGUE. THE PULL OF THE EARTH FALLS HEAVY ON YOUR LIMBS.
NO, WHAT ARE YOU...WAIT! JUST...I KNOW THE SPELL, YOU AMATEUR. IT WON'T WORK ON ME. IT WON'T WO--URKKK!
AMATEUR. PFFT.
YEP. HE CALLED IT, ALL RIGHT.
GO ON, BETHANY. HE CAN'T TOUCH YOU NOW.
NO. HE CAN'T.
YOU HEAR THAT, PHILIP? YOU CAN'T DO ANY MORE SPELLS. AND YOU CAN'T TOUCH ME AT ALL.
BUT I CAN TOUCH YOU.
AND I WILL. UNLESS YOU TAKE AWAY THE SPELL.

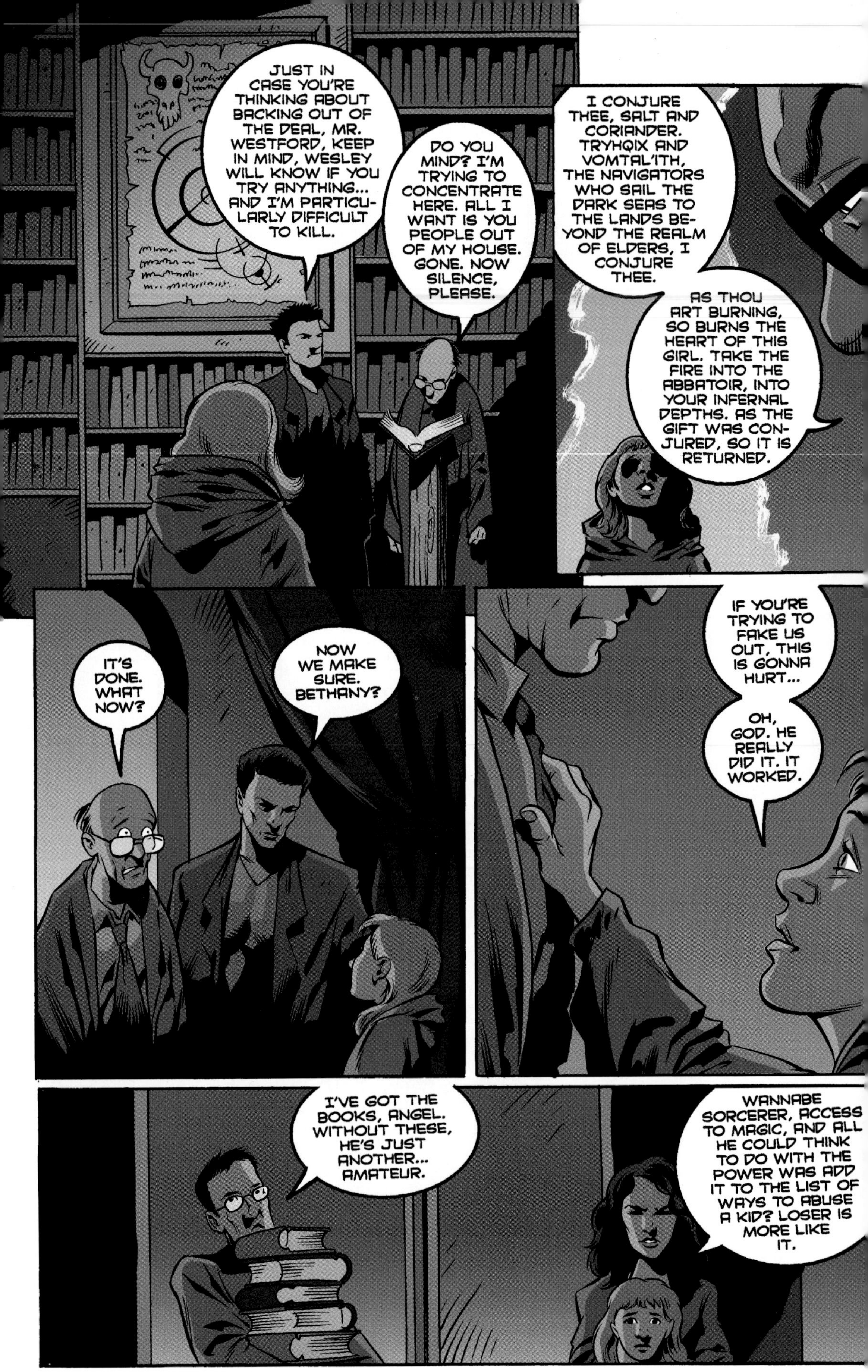
JUST IN CASE YOU'RE THINKING ABOUT BACKING OUT OF THE DEAL, MR. WESTFORD, KEEP IN MIND, WESLEY WILL KNOW IF YOU TRY ANYTHING... AND I'M PARTICULARLY DIFFICULT TO KILL.
DO YOU MIND? I'M TRYING TO CONCENTRATE HERE. ALL I WANT IS YOU PEOPLE OUT OF MY HOUSE. GONE. NOW SILENCE, PLEASE.
I CONJURE THEE, SALT AND CORIANDER. TRYHQIX AND VOMTAL'ITH, THE NAVIGATORS WHO SAIL THE DARK SEAS TO THE LANDS BEYOND THE REALM OF ELDERS, I CONJURE THEE.
AS THOU ART BURNING, SO BURNS THE HEART OF THIS GIRL. TAKE THE FIRE INTO THE ABBATOIR, INTO YOUR INFERNAL DEPTHS. AS THE GIFT WAS CONJURED, SO IT IS RETURNED.
IT'S DONE. WHAT NOW?
NOW WE MAKE SURE. BETHANY?
IF YOU'RE TRYING TO FAKE US OUT, THIS IS GONNA HURT...
OH, GOD. HE REALLY DID IT. IT WORKED.
I'VE GOT THE BOOKS, ANGEL. WITHOUT THESE, HE'S JUST ANOTHER... AMATEUR.
WANNABE SORCERER, ACCESS TO MAGIC, AND ALL HE COULD THINK TO DO WITH THE POWER WAS ADD IT TO THE LIST OF WAYS TO ABUSE A KID? LOSER IS MORE LIKE IT.

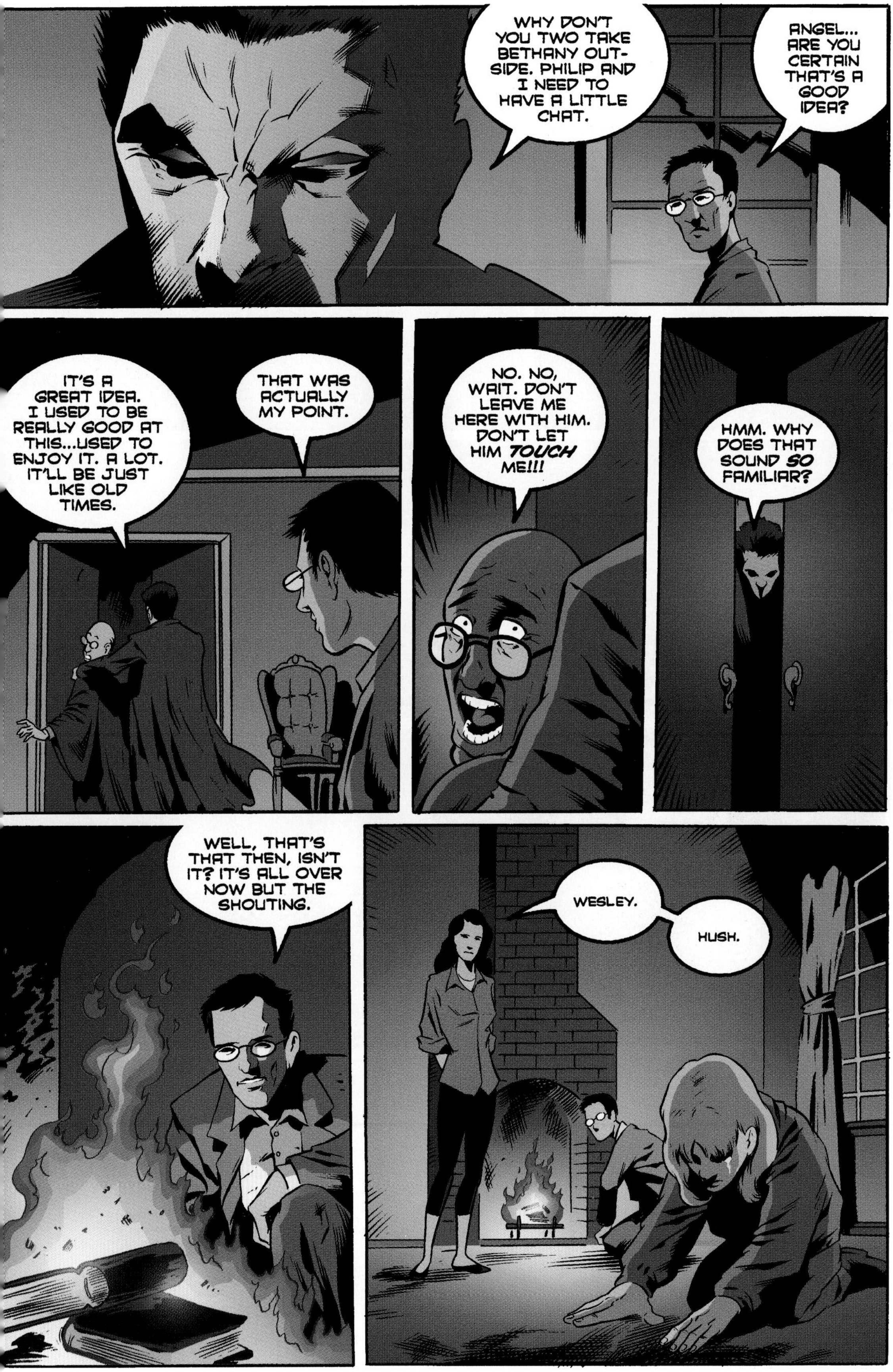
WHY DON'T YOU TWO TAKE BETHANY OUT-SIDE. PHILIP AND I NEED TO HAVE A LITTLE CHAT.
ANGEL... ARE YOU CERTAIN THAT'S A GOOD IDEA?
THAT WAS ACTUALLY MY POINT.
IT'S A GREAT IDEA. I USED TO BE REALLY GOOD AT THIS...USED TO ENJOY IT. A LOT. IT'LL BE JUST LIKE OLD TIMES.
NO. NO, WAIT. DON'T LEAVE ME HERE WITH HIM. DON'T LET HIM *TOUCH* ME!!!
HMM. WHY DOES THAT SOUND *SO* FAMILIAR?
WELL, THAT'S THAT THEN, ISN'T IT? IT'S ALL OVER NOW BUT THE SHOUTING.
WESLEY.
HUSH.

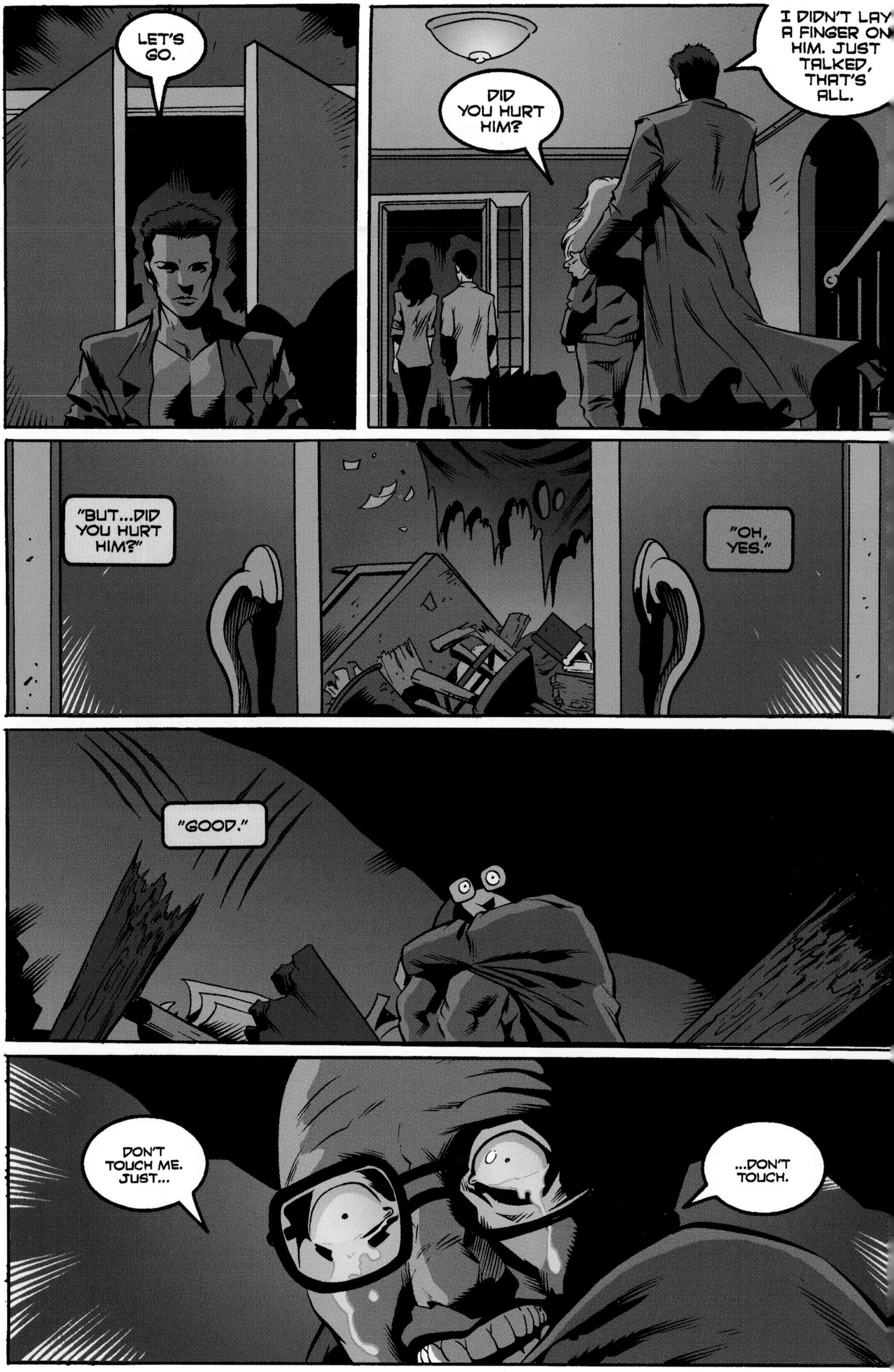
LET'S GO.
DID YOU HURT HIM?
I DIDN'T LAY A FINGER ON HIM. JUST TALKED, THAT'S ALL.
"BUT...DID YOU HURT HIM?"
"OH, YES."
"GOOD."
DON'T TOUCH ME. JUST...
...DON'T TOUCH.

THE END

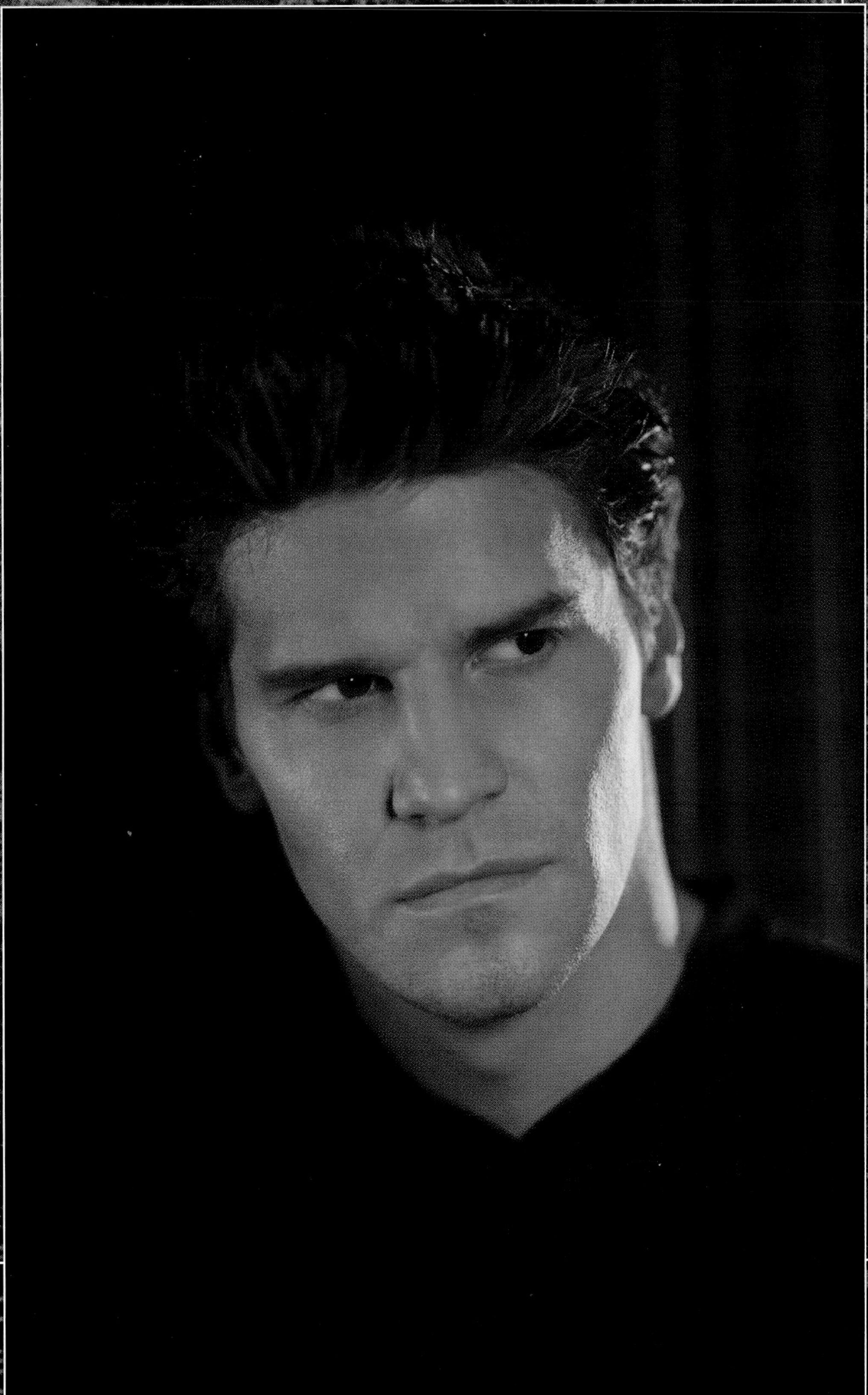

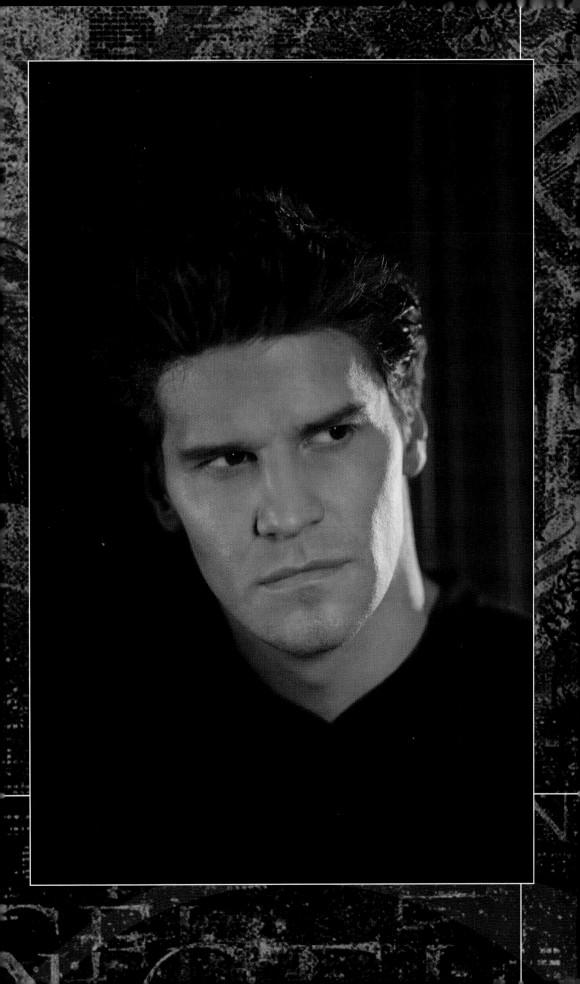

Vampire Slayer trade paperbacks

ANGEL — The Hollower

ANGEL — Surrogates

ANGEL — Earthly Possessions

ANGEL — Hunting Ground

Buffy the Vampire Slayer — The Dust Waltz

Buffy the Vampire Slayer — The Remaining Sunlight

Buffy the Vampire Slayer — the Origin

Buffy the Vampire Slayer — Uninvited Guests

Buffy the Vampire Slayer — Ring of Fire

Buffy the Vampire Slayer — Bad Blood

Buffy the Vampire Slayer — Crash Test Demons

Buffy the Vampire Slayer — Pale Reflections

Buffy the Vampire Slayer — Spike and Dru

Buffy the Vampire Slayer — Food Chain

Buffy the Vampire Slayer — Autumnal

Buffy the Vampire Slayer / Angel — Past Lives

BUFFY THE VAMPIRE SLAYER™, ANGEL™, ALIENS™, AND PREDATOR™ TRADE PAPERBACKS AVAILABLE FROM DARK HORSE COMICS

BUFFY THE VAMPIRE SLAYER

THE DUST WALTZ
Brereton • Gomez • Florea
color paperback
ISBN: 1-56971-342-1 $9.95

THE REMAINING SUNLIGHT
Watson • Bennett • Ketcham
color paperback
ISBN: 1-56971-354-5 $9.95

THE ORIGIN
Golden • Brereton • Bennett • Ketcham
color paperback
ISBN: 1-56971-429-0 $9.95

UNINVITED GUESTS
Watson • Gomez • Florea
color paperback
ISBN: 1-56971-436-3 $10.95

SUPERNATURAL DEFENSE KIT
Watson • Richards • Pimentel
color hardcover w/slipcase
comes with golden-colored cross, "claddagh" ring, and vial of "holy water"
ISBN: 1-56971-486-X $19.95

BAD BLOOD
Watson • Bennett • Ketcham
color paperback
ISBN: 1-56971-445-2 $9.95

CRASH TEST DEMONS
Watson • Richards • Pimentel
color paperback
ISBN: 1-56971-461-4 $9.95

RING OF FIRE
Petrie • Sook
color paperback
ISBN: 1-56971-482-7 $9.95

PALE REFLECTIONS
Watson • Richards • Pimentel
color paperback
ISBN: 1-56971-475-4 $9.95

THE BLOOD OF CARTHAGE
Golden • Richards • Pimentel
color paperback
ISBN: 1-56971-534-3 $12.95

ANGEL

THE HOLLOWER
Golden • Gomez • Florea
color paperback
ISBN: 1-56971-450-9 $9.95

SURROGATES
Golden • Zanier • Owens
color paperback
ISBN: 1-56971-491-6 $9.95

EARTHLY POSSESSIONS
Golden • Sneigoski • Zanier • Owens
color paperback
ISBN: 1-56971-533-5 $9.95

ALIENS

OUTBREAK
Verheiden • Nelson
color paperback
ISBN: 1-56971-174-7 $17.95

NIGHTMARE ASYLUM
Verheiden • Beauvais
color paperback
ISBN: 1-56971-217-4 $16.95

FEMALE WAR
Verheiden • Kieth
color paperback
ISBN: 1-56971-190-9 $16.95

GENOCIDE
Arcudi • Willis • Story
color paperback
ISBN: 1-56971-196-8 $16.95

HARVEST
Prosser • Jones
color paperback
ISBN: 1-56971-198-4 $16.95

ROGUE
Edginton • Simpson
color paperback
ISBN: 1-56971-267-0 $16.95

LABYRINTH
Woodring • Plunkett
color paperback
ISBN: 1-56971-245-X $17.95

STRONGHOLD
Arcudi • Mahnke • Palmiotti
color paperback
ISBN: 1-56971-262-X $16.95

TRIBES
Bissette • Dorman
color hardcover
ISBN: 1-878574-28-0 $24.95

KIDNAPPED
Woodring • Green • Lopez
color paperback
ISBN: 1-56971-372-3 $9.95

APOCALYPSE — THE DESTROYING ANGELS
Schultz • Wheatley
color paperback
ISBN: 1-56971-399-5 $10.95

ALIENS VS PREDATOR

ALIENS VS PREDATOR
Stradley • Norwood • Warner
color paperback
ISBN: 1-56971-125-9 $19.95

THE DEADLIEST OF THE SPECIES
Claremont • Barreto • Guice
color limited hardcover
ISBN: 1-56971-182-8 $99.95

WAR
Stradley • Saltares • Warner
color paperback
ISBN: 1-56971-158-5 $19.95

ETERNAL
Edginton • Maleev
color paperback
ISBN: 1-56971-409-6 $9.95

BATMAN/ALIENS
Marz • Wrightson
color paperback
ISBN: 1-56971-305-7 $14.95

SUPERMAN VS ALIENS
Jurgens • Nowlan
color paperback
ISBN: 1-56971-167-4 $14.95

PREDATOR

CONCRETE JUNGLE
Verheiden • Warner • Randall
color paperback
ISBN: 1-56971-165-8 $14.95

BIG GAME
Arcudi • Dorkin • Gil
color paperback
ISBN: 1-56971-166-6 $14.95

COLD WAR
Verheiden • Randall • Mitchell
color paperback
ISBN: 1-878574-79-5 $13.95

RACE WAR
Vachss • Stradley • Raskin • Pelle
color paperback
ISBN: 1-56971-112-7 $17.95

HELL & HOT WATER
Schultz • Colan
color paperback
ISBN: 1-56971-271-9 $9.95

KINDRED
Lamb • Tolson • O'Connell • Peterson
color paperback
ISBN: 1-56971-270-0 $14.95

PREDATOR VS JUDGE DREDD
Wagner • Alcatena
color paperback
ISBN: 1-56971-345-6 $9.95

TARZAN VS PREDATOR AT THE EARTH'S CORE
Simonson • Weeks
color paperback
ISBN: 1-56971-231-X $12.95

Available from your local comics shop or bookstore!

To find a comics shop in your area, call 1-888-266-4226
For more information or to order direct:
•On the web: www.darkhorse.com •E-mail: mailorder@darkhorse.com
•Phone: 1-800-862-0052 or (503) 652-9701 Mon.-Sat. 9 A.M. to 5 P.M. Pacific Time
*Prices and availability subject to change without notice